THE
SUPREME
GETAWAY

AND OTHER TALES FROM THE PULPS

THE SUPREME GETAWAY

AND OTHER TALES FROM THE PULPS

George Allan England

WILDSIDE PRESS

THE SUPREME GETAWAY
AND OTHER TALES FROM THE PULPS

"Introduction," by John Betancourt is original to this collection and is copyright © 2008 by John Betancourt. "The Supreme Getaway" originally appeared in *People's Magazine*, October 1916. "A Flyer In Junk" originally appeared in *All Story*, March 9, 1918. "The Silo" originally appeared in *Argosy-All Story*, date unknown. "Fire Fight Fire" originally appeared in *Munsey's Magazine*, Vol. 35 (1906). "Speed Limit" originally appeared in *The Cavalier*, November 15, 1913. "The Longest Side" originally appeared in *People's Favorite Magazine* November 10, 1921. "Test Tubes" originally appeared in *Short Stories*, March, 1921. "In Mariners' House" originally appeared in *The Cavalier*, February 7, 1914. "Rough Toss" originally appeared in *Complete Stories*, May 15th, 1932. "Africa" originally appeared in *The Cavalier*, November 1908. "A Worth-While Crime" originally appeared in *Detective Story Magazine*, August 19, 1922

CONTENTS

INTRODUCTION

George Allan England (1877–1936) is mostly remembered these days for his early science-fiction novel, *Darkness and Dawn* (originally published in *Cavalier* magazine as three different serials between 1912 and 1913). Set a thousand years in the future, *Darkness and Dawn* tells the story of a devastated America. Due to its length, it was split into five volumes for paperback publication in the 1960s.

Other works of note include *The Air Trust* (1915), an anticapitalism novel about a monopoly on air travel; *The Golden Blight* (1912), about a ray that transmutes gold into ash; *The Flying Legion* (1920), a near-future (of the time!) tale of the heist of a sacred relic from Mecca; and *The Empire of the Air* (1914), about an invasion by beings from the fourth dimension.

England, however, was a prolific author in many different genres: adventure, romance, mystery, and science fiction were but a few of his themes, as the stories in this volume attest. Here, then are eleven of England's classic pulp stories, ranging from Darkest Africa to the laboratory, from the perils of speed to the perils of savage cannibals! If you haven't encountered George Allan England's work before, you're in for a treat. And if you've already discovered him, chances are high that you've never encountered any of these rare tales before.

Enjoy!

— *John Gregory Betancourt*

THE SUPREME GETAWAY

"SERENE, INDIFFERENT TO FATE." Slatsey leaned back with a sigh of almost perfect bliss in the huge, padded Morris chair, and drew at his priceless panatela.

Dr. Bender, in the depths of a leather rocking chair, his slippered feet on the table, smiled with beatitude.

For their rooms in the extreme privacy of the neat little Hotel de Luxe were marvels of bachelor comfort.

On the table reposed a tray with fragmentary remnants of a delectable feed — always including Pod's ultimate joy, rich rice pudding with lots of butter and cream, and with fat raisins of the juiciest.

"Pretty smooth dump, this," grunted Pod, with another sigh. During the past weeks of inactivity and gorging, he had put on a trifle of forty or fifty pounds.

"Me for the De Looks, every time! Ever since the big gilt dropped into our kicks, after that Vanderpool race, an' we stowed away, I've been strong for the resher-shay stuff they hand out here. The way they act certainly makes a hit with muh!"

"And no fly-cops butting in, either," added Ben. "I tell you, Pod, this con-throwing isn't such a much, beside the real refinements of a home like this. Now that we've brought home the bunting, me for squaring it, a bundle of A-1 bonds, and respectability.

"That's my dope — that, and a continuation of this chow, with a little something dry on the side. What more could a couple of honest, retired congents require?"

Pod sighed again, still more deeply; but this sigh held less of happiness than the first.

Bender's reference to "home" had stirred the smoldering coals of a new sentiment in his huge heart — love-coals, now being blown upon by Birdy McCue.

And in Pod's disturbed mind visions began to rise. Not even the memories of rice and raisins could quite smother the growing flame.

Birdy was the pals' own particular waitress. Her complexion was of cream and rose-petals, her eyes a May-sky blue, her luxuriant hair a yellow wherein no H2O2 had ever mingled its corrupting influence.

Birdy's bare arm was firm and rounded and very white, also her V-cut waitress's shirtwaist disclosed a full throat, and her apron-straps rested over a more than Junoesque bosom.

In addition to all this, an occasional glimpse of her ankle as she swung in and out the double-doors of the dining room disclosed it to be of that trim and silk-stockinged variety which oft-times leads to reveries.

In fine, Birdy was one buxom, healthy, beautiful young woman, full of life and the joy of life, weighing-one hundred and forty-two, age twenty-five, ripe and fair — yes, a peach.

Pod sighed for the third time, very heavily, and forgot to smoke. Had his rubicund face been capable of it, he would have paled slightly.

Ben shot a quick, keen glance at him, by the mellow light of the frosted electric table-lamp. His brow wrinkled. Did he, too, sigh; or was it an extra deep inhalation of the perfumed cigarette-smoke he loved so well?

Pod noticed neither the look nor the possible sigh of his running-mate. For he was thinking — of Birdy; pondering on the blissful existence of the past few weeks, so warm, well-fed, and secure, disturbed only by the gnawings of the insistent love-bug which, its period of . . . incubation now past, was beginning to bite in real earnest.

He was mentally reviewing the situation. He had, well he knew, made no false step; he felt himself in favor with his Juno.

The first day at the De Luxe he had slipped her a five-spot, from an obese roll.

"This is just kind of a starter, kid," he had remarked nonchalantly. "I'm an extensive feeder, an' I want you to remember me. I can talk to a chicken egg cassy-roll louder than any man in Manhat.

"I can reach further an' stab a pie deeper than a Mafia knifing a snitch, an' I hold the international rice-puddin' long-distance record, bar none.

"Crab-meat is where I live, see? I'll stow away grouse and truffles against all comers. Are you on? You be the fixin' kid and keep things comin'; shove a little chick lunch up to the room every p.m. about eleven; let me do the bill o' fare through, an' repeat, an' you'll gather. Got it?"

"I'm on!" she had smiled with a dazzle of white teeth. "And your friend?"

"Oh, him? Say, he's dyspeptic. A good fella, you know, but — It's me that's the bear on eats. So chase 'em in lively, kiddo, and — you know!"

Birdy had remembered, and had chased 'em in. Every night, too, the tray had come up to No. 18 with succulent dainties piled; and not once had there been dearth of sugared rice-pudding and raisins simply bursting with juice.

And the love-bug, hidden among all those ambrosial dainties, had bitten deep. Now Pod was simply one vast culture-medium for the virus. Every ounce of his three hundred and fifty-seven pounds was potentially enamored of a goddess who could steer such eats to him. Which made the case extremely serious.

"Say, Ben!"

"Huh?"

Pod only shifted uneasily in the huge chair, and sucked at his smoke, which had gone out.

"Oh, nothin'," he mumbled. "I was just thinkin', that's all."

About a week after this first faint flapping of the wings of self-exposition, a wonderful September moon, full and round and golden, shone through the heat of the city haze and flooded the windows of the pals' sitting room. They sat smoking, lights out, with their feet on the sill; and the magic of the night, the orb, the breeze, stirred Slats to confidences.

"Say, Ben," he commenced once more, embarrassed as a schoolboy. He could face the world with a smile, and "con" it without batting an eye; but to open his huge heart to his pal caused the sweat to bead his brow. Uneasily he mopped it. "Ben?"

"Huh?"

"Say — you an' me — we — you know."

"Know what? Uneasy? Want to beat out on the pike again, and put the trimming tools to work once more? Forget it! All off, Bo! We —"

"Back up! You're in wrong! You an' me, we've been runnin'-mates now for ten or twelve years. We've nicked high an' panhandled low. Sometimes we've been on the outside, lookin' in, sometimes the reverse.

"We've got ours in about every known country in the world, an' some unknown countries; we've laid on velvet an' again on the rods. Our little mob of two has certainly been some swell mob, an' you've been one classy pal, but — well —"

"Well, what?" demanded Ben, with a sharp, half-guilty glance at the huge bulk beside him in the moonlight. "What you got on your chest?"

"I — this — I mean, this single life proposition ain't the silky frame-up it's touted to be, after all," Pod continued hoarsely.

"When a gink is young an' everythin's fallin' his way, he naturally rolls away from anythin' permanent in the skirt line. *All* right! But when the ivories begins to shy off and the noble brow begins to connect with the neck, right over the dome of the bean — aw, nothin' to it, kid, nothin' to it!"

Slats made an out-sweep with his huge fist, as though to drive dull bachelorhood away, and sighed powerfully. "It's then a man gets ripe to tumble for something smooth in the she-line, Ben! It's then he's the fall guy for the cozy home idea! Say! Ain't *you* never framed it, what? Ain't you never fell for none o' this here cream stuff, yourself?"

Ben only shifted uneasily in his chair, and grunted something unintelligible.

One might have thought a sudden chill of hostility had all at once fallen over him; but if so, Slats took no heed. Instead, with a rapt smile at the moon and a new timbre in his mighty voice, he went on resistlessly:

"Love, ah, love! It's some best bet, believe *me*. It's a right steer, an' no come-back! Love builds the cottage where the birds do a warble an' they's ivy round the door, like in them illustrated songs, Ben.

"Love comes across with the prattle of innocent voices an' the patter of feet that ain't never hiked on no White Ways. Love greets you at the door with a glad fin, after you've had the rough toss outside.

"It bats you on the knob with baby mitts an' whispers 'Dad!' in your receiver. It sets on your knee an' hands you a kiss, front o' the fireplace when the snow is blowin' outside. Oh, it's the smooth proposition, kid, surest thing you know!"

"Uh-huh?"

"Nix on this rovin', Ben! Nix, not, no more! No more raw deals. All it means is, even hidin' up like here, always afraid somebody's goin' to cook us, after all.

"It means stir, in time; a slip-up, somewhere, some day; and for a finish, the slab an' the table. I been thinkin', kid, thinkin' long an' hard.

"Me for the happy home, the family, the peachy frau, the lawn-mower, hose, garden, an' all thereto appertain-in'. An' when it's time to blow my light out, no crocus carvin' me an' no pine board, but a right pebble over me, plumb respectable, Ben — past all squared an' forgotten — A-1 turn-out with a dozen hacks, an' the 'Sacred to the Memory of' just as big as any of 'em!"

Pause. Silence. In the moonlight a close observer could have perceived the huge fellow's Adam's-apple working convulsively, while a tear gleamed in his blinking eye.

Ben seemed pondering. Up to the pals, from the asphalted side street, rose a clack-clack-clack of hoofs. A trolley-gong clashed on the avenue, and, farther off, the roar of an L train broke the evening calm.

Ben, his face very grim, yet with a certain air of relief, tossed his cigar out of the window and turned toward his side-partner.

"Straight dope?" he demanded sternly. "No phony gag, but the real thing?"

"Realest ever! I got the love-bug, kid. It's put this con life of ours on the fritz, for fair! I'm goin' to square it, an' be a hick, myself. Why? You ain't peeved with me, are you?"

"Peeved nothing! Delighted! Here, let me mitt you, old boy. Go to it!"

Ben thrust out his hand, which Pod wrung with a sudden burst of gratitude and affection.

"That's the way to pass it out!" exclaimed the big fellow, in a choking voice. "I been leary of pullin' it on you, kid, 'cause I didn't know but you'd sit up and howl. But I see now —"

"You're on. Congratulations! Fact is, old boy, the same idea has been flagging me, too, some time past. Only I didn't hardly dare to pull it on you. But now —"

"*You?*" blurted Pod, gaping. "You stung, too? My Gawd! So then, if we split, it'll be O. K. on both sides, an' both of us in the clover-bed? Fine! Who's the skirt, Ben? Who, what, an' where?"

A knock on the door interrupted this heart-to-heart.

"Come!" boomed Slats.

A bellhop appeared with the usual evening tray, neatly over-spread with a spotless damask. As though well used to the task, he switched on the light, and deftly spread the festive board on the pals' center table.

The two old friends and co-grafters watched the proceedings with satisfaction. Evidently, love as yet had not advanced to the stage where appetite had begun to fail.

His work done, the hop departed. Pod and Ben drew up to the bounteous feast, but something was on the big fellow's mind. He gazed on the pudding and shook his head, then glanced at his pal inquiringly.

"Ben?"

"What?"

"You didn't know I was some writer, did you?"

Ben, just unfolding his napkin, stared in amazement.

"Writer? Scratch-work, or how?"

"No, billy-doo's. Say, Ben, I — I don't feel like the eats till I've got this off my chest, like. I want you to listen to this here letter I've doped out for — for *her*, you tumble.

"Listen, an' then throw me the straight spiel. Is it the right goods or ain't it? Is it billed to make a center-shot an' ring the bell, the weddin'-bell, or — or is it a frosty freeze? Is —"

"You mean you've been framing some love-stuff?"

Slats nodded.

"Just hold back on the feeds till you let this trickle into your think-tank," he adjured, producing a folded sheet of scented lavender paper from his breast pocket, left side, nearest the cardiac apparatus.

"Go ahead and fire!" exclaimed Ben, eagerly eying the tray.

"All right, kid. Now, you just listen to *some* proposal!"

Hotel de Luxe,

Today and Every Day.

MY OWN HUMMINGBIRD! MY BUNCH OF VELVET TAFFY!

Oh, you kid! This is to Wise you that you have certainly Put one over hard on Yours Forever. For many years I thought I never would Kick in on this here Love whirl, but you have Sloughed me for fair. To say you are the Goods, is putting it so feeble it's almost an insult. When I gaze upon you, I am just Nuts to tear into the Sweet Home racket, with Ivy round the door. Do you get me, Hun?

I am truly Dippy to throw my Net over you and cop yon off, all for my lonesome. I've got the strong Hunch we could lope to where the Roses bloom and the robins nest again, and you would be my Dove and I would be your Pouter pigeon for life.

"Say, Ben, ain't that some poetical?"

You are my great, big beautiful Doll, believe me! This is no needle monologue, but the goods, and I have the Wad to back it. The first time I ever Lamped you, it was a knockout, and I took the mat for ten. I could see you Coming, even then, and ever since, you've been Getting it on me, worse and more of it, Now, Dear heart, don't Crab a loving soul by no icy Mitt gag, for believe me, though I may not be such a Romeo to look at, my heart and Bundle are in the right place.

I know I could carry some class, myself, with you for a running-mate. When I get my front on, I'm not half hard to behold. And I'm strictly on the Level in this deal, no Phony. You tie up to me, and you'll know you've got a real man, no Shrimp half portions, but the 18-K article.

> *The Rose is red, the Grass is green,*
> *You are my Queen,*
> *The fairest ever Seen,*
> *So be mine, or I'll repine,*
> *Be my Love, my beautiful Dove,*
> *And forever I'll be true to you,*
> *With Ivy twining round the door!*

Pod paused, breathing heavily, and swabbed his brow with a napkin.

"How about it, kid?" he demanded anxiously. "Is it the goods, or ain't it? Poetry, too!"

"Some literature, all right!" asserted Ben, gazing away, "But do you think 'you' and 'door' make an O. K. rime? 'You' and 'in the stew' would go, but —"

Slats snorted with disgust.

"Stew, you lob!" he cried. "That shows how much poetic feelin' you got! Why, this here's blank verse, the last two lines. Blank verse! That's the swellest kind!"

"Oh, that's so, too. I forgot. It's blank, all right. Yes, it's the goods. Any more?"

"Some! And it ought to be the hot stuff, too. Took me the best part of ten days to frame it! There's better comin', too. Just take a slant at *this*, will you?"

If you think you could fall for me, Kiddo, say the word and you're on, for life! Cupid has went and handed you my whole flock of goats, that's no pipe. What do you say we bunch our play, from now on? You'd sure be some Classy pal for me! Any time you want to frame up with me, working Double harness, I'm your Pippin. Can't you see me, Dovey? If we hitch, I know we can give the Census and the course of Human events a right Sassy push, all right, so don't Shy off. But be my Molasses Bunch, till death us do pry Apart!

All I ask is your Heart and hand, and a Continuation of the swell Eats, as per this last month.

Ben started suddenly, with a quick glance at Pod, but the latter was far too absorbed in his reading to notice anything.

No use for you to be a side stem in this Hashery, when you can be the main tent in a Cottage with Ivory — Ivy — round the door. Shed that apron, kid, and I'll show you the real silks, cut on the Bias, with fringe and doll-fixings all from Paris. Get me? Cut out the tay-ta-tay confabs with that fresh new Night clerk, same

as I've been wise to, the past Week, and accept a Loving heart
that beats only for you.

Ben leaned forward, his face darkening, fist clenched, and eyes staring. His mouth was set in a thin line. Pod blissfully pursued the letter.

Your blue lamps and hair and the Way you Double up on the
rice pudding have won my heart, Baby. The coin I've staked you
to, for that stock-game, and the eats-money I've slipped you, is
only a taste beside what I'll slide your way when we're Hitched,
So say the word, and —

The letter was never finished, for with a wordless cry Ben started up. His fist fell on the table with a bang. The dishes rattled. A cup fell crashing to the floor.

Pod, startled, dropped the letter and stared, wide-eyed.

"Wh — wh — why, what th —" he stammered blankly.

"You — *you!*" hissed Ben, shaking a passionate forefinger right under Pod's nose. "So *that's* your game, is it, you scab? *Rat!* You — I —"

"For Gawd's sake, Ben!"

"Copping my girl right under my very eyes, you sneak!"

"Your — *your* —"

"Yes, mine! For three weeks now —"

"But — first thing we blew in here, Ben, I slid her a V! Every week since, another one! An' I've slipped her coin for a stock-deal she's in — an' these here classy feeds she sends up are all for me, an' she's mine —"

"Ah-ha! So, eh?" Ben's fist shook violently in the huge fellow's astonished face. "So? But we'll see about that, we'll see! These feeds are for you, are they? Why, you poor boob, they're mine! Ten a week she's had from me — ten bucks per, you tumble? An' as for the deal in stocks —"

"*You* been touched, too?"

"Have I? Why, sure! But — I didn't know you — you — had! Why— er — see here, Pod —"

"Huh?"

Ben's fist fell, and over his pale face a strange expression passed. His eyes sought Pod's, and for the space of ten heartbeats their looks met in silence.

At last Ben spoke:

"Pod!"

"Ben?"

"Whoa, back! Back up, both of us!"

"You mean —"

Pod was leaning forward now, gripping the table-edge with a fat though powerful hand. On his brow the sweat had started thicker than ever, and his breath was coming hard.

"Ben, you mean we — we're in wrong?"

"Wrong — dead wrong, so help me! There's more behind all this soft-soap biz and all this swell night-lunch racket than we're wise to yet.

"Pod, we're being played against each other, both ends toward the middle! A skirt is trying to do the oceana roll over us and con each of us into thinking we're *it*!

"I had it all doped to land solid with Birdy two or three weeks ago. So did you. Each of us has been passing the gilt to her —"

"Don't, Ben — don't!" Pod's eyes were leaking and he stretched out an imploring hand. "I'm wise a plenty, so cut that explanation stuff! But — it hurts, Ben; hurts like — jus' same; when I had it all doped I was goin' to bust into married bliss — ivy round the door —"

"No more o' that now! We're both leery, now we've got a peek at the works. Just a throw-off she was steering us, Pod — that's all. How big a haymow of the green has she raked off you already?"

"Oh, maybe four, five hundred — on Consolidated Copper. She said her cousin in Wall Street —"

"I'm in for a thousand. Only it was her uncle!"

"Ben! An' we, we are — supposed to be — the smoothest con-workers in the U. S. A. or out!"

Bender stared a moment, then burst into a laugh of mingled bitterness and relief.

"My feed I thought it was all the time!" he cried. "You thought it was yours. Both wrong — just as wrong as in our size-up of Birdy and her affections. Who's nuts now? Pod, Bender & Co.! And the answer is —"

Pod Slattery arose, with all the dignity of his three hundred and fifty-seven pounds, and faced his old-time pal. In his eyes still gleamed the dew of heartfelt disappointment, but his lips were smiling as he spoke.

"Ben, old boss," said he, "the answer is, a new deal and reorganization of the film on a long lease Birdy's. smooth O. K.

"We've let a skirt near trim us and if it gets out our rep ain't worth a hoot in Tophet. She's no ordinary poke-getter or cold hand worker, Birdy ain't. No, this was no penny ante game she was up to, she was stakin' to make a kill, what with all them kind woids an' — an' juicy raisins an' cream —

"A classy hex, all right aimin' to fetch down a big bundle when she had us hog tied right. In a while longer she'd had our whole roll an' us spoutin' our sparks for pad-money! Oh an onion, kid! But now we're hep — an' it's one big hike for ours!"

" 'Hike'!" echoed Ben enthusiastically. "The quicker, the sooner — far, far away!"

"Pack your keister!" Pod directed dramatically, with a sweep of his arm. "This very night we flit! See her again after all them ivy visions? Nix! Us for the big getaway, P.D.Q!

"I can't pull much of this here sentimental stuff on friendship, kid, but you know what I mean."

"That time you dug me out o' Sing Sing I ain't passin' up. No, nor the times we carried the banner in India, did a Marathon on the African veldt, dodged a smash in Yokohama, an' — an all the hundreds of other times, some velvet, some sand paper, we been through together.

"What? Let a peek-a-boo and a hobble pry us apart? Nix not! We must ha' been pipes, Ben, you an' me, to even think it! All over kid! It's you an' me again, with no Buttinskies, to the finish! An' my mitt to bind it!" In silence Ben took the huge and generous hand. For a minute their eyes met. Then Pod turned away.

"Ivy, hell," he whispered under his breath and with a kind of savage joy began routing his effects out of closet and chiffonier and hurling them into his suitcase.

Untouched, the tempting night lunch stood on the table. The

savory pot of tea grew cold, the sherbet melted, and the fat raisins oozed out their juice forsakenly into the thick cream, which now had lost all its charm.

Half an hour later an envelope lay on the table, addressed to the hotel management. Within it reposed coin of the realm to pay the bill up to and including the following Saturday night.

Down the fire escape, meanwhile, Pod, Ben, and the suitcases wended their way to the alley at the rear of the hotel.

And the friendly September night received them; and the great world opened out once more ahead of them — the world of ventures and of games, of losses and of winnings, of honest grafts and touches — best of all, of friendship and the brotherhood of long-tried pals.

Damon and Pythias, David and Jonathan, Pylades and Orestes, Nisus and Euryalus had nothing on these two incomparable running mates as they hailed a taxi on the avenue and sped toward the Grand Central in time for the Bombshell Limited for Chicago and all points West.

Midnight found them still consuming fat cigars in the luxurious smoking-compartment of the Pullman and basking in the newfound joy of freshly consolidated partnership.

"Some getaway this time!" murmured Ben, lighting another panatela. "Speaking of narrow cracks, this latest riffle sure has all past performances riveted to the post. I *seem* to be sitting on a leather cushion, bo; but really I'm down on all fours, thanking Heaven!"

Pod smiled, drew from his pocket a scented, lavender sheet of paper, set it afire with a match and with it fired up afresh his smoldering cigar. He held the paper carefully till it was but a crinkling bit of black, run through with crawling sparks.

Then with great precision and gusto he dropped it into the cuspidor.

Leaning back with a huge sigh of comfort and relief he exhaled a cloud of smoke and cheerfully contemplated the roof in eloquent silence.

The pals' great joy would without fail have leaped up one thousand per cent had they known this simple fact, viz.: that in the rice pudding on the table, back in the De Luxe, reposed at that moment enough chloral hydrate or knock-out drops to have put them sound asleep for many hours.

The drops had been considerately added unto the pudding by said Birdy McCue, in view of a large prospective reward from the new night-clerk, who — let me tell you confidentially — was none other than William J. Shearns of the Cosmos Detective Agency, which had long "wanted" them for several little matters.

"Where ignorance is bliss," eh?

You're on!

A FLYER IN JUNK

THE STOUT, EXPANSIVE MAN with the pompadour lighted still another cigar, leaned back against the leather cushion of the Pullman, smiling.

"As a deal, it was some deal, believe *me*!" he remarked, contemplating the serious-looking man with the horn spectacles, who sat opposite. "It ain't every day o' the week you can pull off a stunt like that, an' get away with it!"

"You say the guy that fell for it, and that you wished the old boat off onto, claimed to be wise to cars?" asked the young fellow in the striped suit, inhaling a lungful of Egyptian smoke.

"An' then some!" chuckled the stout man. "He wasn't after it, for himself. No, he was buyin' for another guy — man by the name of Robinson, from Boston. The way he put it to me, this Robinson didn't claim to be no Solomon in the buzz-buggy-business. Didn't trust his own judgment in buyin' no second-hand wagon, an' so got him to O.K. the machine. That's what makes me laugh, even now, when I think of it!"

The stout man cachinnated, and blew smoke. He of the horn spectacles fixed an interested gaze upon him.

"'I know 'em from tires to top,' says this duck, when he comes to give Liz the once-over. Liz was her name. Just Liz. 'What I say to Robinson, goes. I have *cart blonk*,' says he. Well, when I got through with him, it wasn't *cart blonk* he had, but cart junk. Say! They don't slip anything much over on Jimmy Dill — that's me!"

"Was she really on the fritz?" asked the young fellow, while the serious-looking man lent an interested ear.

"Fritz? You said somethin'! Fritziest ever! She was an old Buick model seventeen, to begin with, crop of 1912. Seven-pass., rebuilt to runabout shape. Sixth-hand when I got her from a guy that had gave her up in despair. I paid him a hundred an' give him five three-dollar meal-tickets in my cafe. I run the Alarm Cafe in Revere, see? Battleship gray, she was. Sixty H. P., with cylinders as big as pails, an' took a pail o' gas, too, every time she coughed."

"Some baby, eh?" inquired the young man, with approbation.

"Oh, boy! Two men to crank her — one to throw her an' the other to hold his hand over the intake — an' throwin' her was a Sandow job, or a Gotch, at that. You had to pump up the gas by hand, every few miles, when the pump was working, which it most usually wasn't, an' then you'd stall till you got her patched. An' no emergency. Only a foot brake; an' one time she busted her universal on the downgrade in a traffic-jam. An' maybe I didn't sweat blood, skiddin' her through — but she coasted right to a garage an' stopped outside, an' all they had to do was come out an' haul her in!"

"So you sold her, did you?" interrogated the horn spectacles. "Unloaded her on some sucker?"

"*Did* I? But wait till I tell you some more about her. She had her faults, even when I got her, a-plenty. But travel? Say! I never did dare open her up, full. When she really got goin' — an' sometimes she could be started in less 'n fifteen minutes — why, there wasn't no such things as hills to her. She went wild, simply wild over hills. An' on the level stretches she dusted 'em all, Just a gray streak. Zowie! Never needed no horn, nor nothin'. Make a noise like a pewmatic riveter on a jag. Hear her two-mile off. *Some* boat!"

Jimmy Dill puffed smoke-arrows, heavily, and nodded strong confirmation. The serious-looking man's interest seemed growing ever greater. Dill continued with enthusiasm:

"Liz was good, 'spite of all her kick-ups, till last spring. Then she slumped sudden, though she still kept flyin'. She was a flyer, even if she begun to show signs of bein' junk. Tires begun to go bad, with a slow leak in one that we couldn't fix, noway — all wearin' down, an' no more o' them bolted-on kind to be had. One lug of her cylinder-casin' cracked off, too. That was bad. Supposin' another went, while she was doin' sixty, an' the engine dropped out? Flowers for yours truly.

"Magneto went on the blink, too, an' cylinders wore crooked, so oil worked up, an' she'd only run a few miles hittin' on four. Then she begin coughin' till you'd clean the plugs again. Who the devil can clean plugs every five miles? Her feed got leakin', too, so you couldn't pump her up without lamin' yourself. An' her gearshift busted, some way or 'nother, so for a while she'd only run on low — I once brought her home, sixteen mile, on low — an' then all of a sudden she'd only run on high. After a lot o' tinkerin', we got her to run on low an' high, but no second. An' boy! The times I used to have, tryin' to coax her from low to high!

"I begun to think I'd have to scrap her. But it was only after her radiator blew out, while I was to Ellengone out in the country, an' I had to plug it with chewin' gum, an' then she took to back-firin', an' I had to be towed in by a fliv, on the end of thirty foot o' barb-wire that we cut off'n a farmer's fence, that I phoned Levitsky.

"Levitsky, the junkman, come an' said fifty beans on the hoof, as she stood. I was strong for the fifty, but Bill Hemingway, friend o' mine — he's in the garridge business, Bill is — says I can maybe do better. So I canned Levitsky an' put an ad in the paper, no price set. An' several guys come an' give her the o.o., an' then blow. Till at last this here wise duck, sent by this here Robinson, arrives.

II.

"I HAS LIZ already runnin' an' I'm loaded for bear, when he shows up, 'cause he's already phoned me he's comin', an' I'm not takin' no chances on not bein' able to start her. It's kind of noisy, down by the Alarm Cafe, with lots of electrics and et cet, so Liz don't sound so awful conspicuous. She's all washed an' polished, anyhow, an' that's half a sale. The wise duck gives her the up-an'-down, an' then he says, says he:

"'Demonstrate her, will you?'

"'Demonstrate is my middle name,' says I. 'All goods strictly as represented, or no sale. I wouldn't take a dollar of any man's money on no false misrepresentations,' I says. 'Money back if not sound an' kind. Get right in, mister, an' we'll hop to it!'

"So the wise guy gets in, an' I prepares to make Liz do or die, or perish in the attempt.

"I has her all loaded for bear, o' course, like I said before. Got enough gas pumped inta the tank on the dash to last her five mile, an' the plugs all clean, an' tires all pumped hard — I'm prayin' harder than the tires is, they won't blow — an' I got a new set o' batt'ries in, an' got her wired so that when I let on to throw her onta the mag., she'll still be on bats. The mag.'s out o' commission, total.

"An' I has her on the stiff down-grade front o' the cafe, so she'll slip from low inta high, without makin' no kick-up. So that's all right. So he's gets in, the wise duck does, an' away we blows.

"Half-way down the grade, I shift her an' get away with it, O. K. The noisy street camouflages the kick-up in the engine so it ain't very raw. I pushes her out onta the boulevard, an' lets her out, an' boy! Does she hike? Some! The wise duck has to take his dicer off an' hold it in his lap, to keep it, an' the way we passes everythin' is a wonder.

"So far, it's pie with ice-cream on top, but my heart's in my mouth about the big hill. Everybody always has to go into second, on that doggone hill, you see, an' Liz ain't got no second. I try to turn off toward the beach road, but the wise duck says, 'No, let's try her out on the hill,' so that's all off. So I decides I'll try to rush the hill, an' trust to prayer an' luck, when flap-flap-flap somethin' begins goin', on her right hind leg.

"'What's that?' asks the w. d., anxious.

"'Oh, nothin',' says I, easy-like. 'She's maybe picked up a piece o' hoop, or a lath, or somethin'.'

"'Better stop an' have a look, hadn't you?'

"I'm sweatin' blood. If I stop, I can't never make that hill, an' if I don't, Lord knows what'll bust. I takes chances — there ain't nothin' else to do — an' charges the hill. Man! How noble old Liz answers me! Up an' over she goes, full lung-power, an' straightens out on the level again. Whew! But there's more sweat on my manly brow than what the thermometer could account for!"

"You had a hard time disposing of your bunch of fossilized pig-iron, on a guarantee to return the money if not as represented, didn't you?" inquired the gentleman with the horn glasses, a bit cynically. "Your narrative interests me, decidedly. What happened next?"

"Next? Oh, after we're over the top, I stops Liz on a good startin' grade, jumps out, an' finds one tire's gettin' ready to lay down on the job an' die. There's a long strip o' rubber, loose, that's been whackin' against the mudguard. I yanks it off, drops it in the road an' climbs back, smilin', though my heart's half-dead, 'cause that there tire's liable to blow worse 'n a whale, any old time, an' I got no spare.

"'Well, what was it?' asks the w. d.

"'Oh, nothin' — piece of a barrel-hoop,' says I.

"'Puncture?'

"'Naw! These here tires is puncture-proof, anyhow,' I says, an' away we slides, again. But all the time I'm watchin' the speedometer careful an' anxious, 'cause if my five miles o' gas runs out, I'm done. So, pretty soon, I rounds back towards town, again. An' now Liz begins to skip. Three's all she'll hit on.

"'Hello,' says the w. d. 'What now?'

"'Nothin' at all.' I assures him, smilin' confidential. 'Dirty plug. *That* don't signify. Ain't been cleaned in six months. She's some little bearcat to travel, ain't she?'

"The duck allows she is, an' so there's no more said. I'm prayin' hard we'll reach the cafe without no traffic hold-up. If I ever have to go inta low, I'm done. Once she's on low, on level ground, you couldn't get her inta high with dynamite. But Liz's luck holds. Nothin' jams us. An' so, pretty soon, there we are again, back front o' the cafe, with her nose downhill. I makes a snappy stop with the foot brake an' crams her wheel against the curb, to hold her from runnin' away.

"'Why don't you put on your emergency?' asks the duck.

"I only scorns him.

"'Emergency, nothin'!' says I. 'No such animal, on *this* boat. She's a racin' car, stripped light. I thought you said you was hep to cars, tires to top!'

"That settles the duck. He climbs out, puts on his hat, shoves his mitts down in his pockets, an' looks wise.

"'Well, mister,' says. I, 'can she travel, or can't she?'

"'She sure can, but —'

"'Is she some classy boat, or ain't she? What?'

"'Classy is right,' he answers, while Bill Hemingway, who's been layin' in the offin', so to speak, lays off from layin' in the offin' an' lays alongside. Bill assumes a flankin' position, to reinforce me. 'She's classy, speedy an' all that,' the duck says, 'but — well —'

"'No well to it!' I interrupts, lookin' at my watch as if I had a dozen dates. 'You gotta talk turkey to me, right off the bat. I got six offers, already. There's only one one boat like this here, in the world,' says I, which is strictly true, 'an' it's the lucky man that gets her,' which is what I call a flight of imagination. 'She's liable to be gone in an hour. What's your best offer?'

"'Hundred an' fifty,' says the w. d.

"My mouth's just openin' to yell: 'Gimme it!,' when Bill, he horns in with: "'Nothin' doin'!' His tone's indignant. 'I guess not! Nix on the one-fifty. Say, I wouldn't let my own brother have it for no such slaughter price!'

"'What's your lowest?' asks the w. d., anxious.

"I'm just goin' to bust inta tears an' fall on my knees, implorin' Bill to keep out an' not grab me from drawin' down three times what Liz is worth even for junk, but he elbows me out. The duck squints at Liz, an' then says, says he:

"'I'm not buyin' for myself, you understand, but for a friend o' mine, name o' Robinson. What's your very lowest?'

"'Name a figure yourself,' says Bill, cool as one o' my frozen puddin's. 'You know the car. You've had a full demonstration, an' she's all as represented. She's just as you see her, an' no comeback if purchased. Ever see a boat any classier?'

"'Oh, she's good, all right.'

"'As an expert, now I ask you, is she the goods or ain't she?'

"'She can travel, I admit. She's certainly there!'

"'Name a figure!'

"'One sixty-five, an' that's the last cent I'll go!'

"'Mister, you've bought a car!' says Bill, holdin' out his hand. 'Congratulations!'

"Somethin' kind of seems to rise up an' cloud my sight, like I was faintin'. When I comes to, gets my eyes open again an' catches my breath — when I comes up for air, you might say — the duck is diggin' up eight new twenties an' all. I'm still gaspin', like, but Bill shoves me into the camouflage, or the background, or somethin', while the duck climbs inta Liz.

"'Good luck,' says Bill, wavin' his hand, as Liz slides away down hill. 'Here's hopin' Robinson will find her sound an' kind, an' be as glad to get her as we're glad to do him a favor an' let him have her. I congratulate you on havin' bought the only car in the world like her — the only original Liz. Good luck an' goodby!'

"Away the duck goes, down the hill an' round the corner, with Liz still hittin' on three an' the slow leak bringin' one front tire nearly flat, an' now an' then back-firin' like a Krupp. An' that's the last I ever see or either the Duck or Liz. I never sees Robinson, nor hear of him, neither. He's a game sport an' a good loser, I'll say that for him. Ain't he? What?"

The young man in the striped suit nodded, grinning. The man with the horn-glasses looked very thoughtful, very grave. A little silence fell in the smoking-compartment, while from the engine sounded a long whistle, announcing an approaching stop.

"Great stuff!" suddenly exclaimed the young man, with enthusiasm, as he slapped his knee. "That's the best put-over I ever heard, in the boat line!" He turned to the man in the horn glasses. "Well, what d'you think of it? You don't seem to fall for it very strong, do you?"

"No, I don't," answered the man in the horn spectacles. "As a matter of fact, I'm Robinson!"

III.

THE MAN with the pompadour stared vacantly. His jaw dropped.

"Good *night*!" he cried. "*You*?"

"I have that honor, sir."

"Go on! You ain't the guy that the wise duck bought Liz for?"

The gentleman with the horn glasses drew out his card-case, looked it through, chose a card and presented it.

"At your service," he answered.

He of the pompadour read:

WILLIAM F. ROBINSON
Attorney-at-Law
27 Pearl St., Boston

For a moment, the blankest silence fell that had ever permeated that smoking-compartment. Then Pompadour gulped, wiping his brow with a tremulous hand:

"Good night! I — I sure spilled the beans that time!"

"The beans, sir, are certainly spilled," answered Horn Glasses. "The entire pot-full. And that is not all. Now that I know the complete inside story of the infamous fraud perpetrated on me, the same constituting a clear case of obtaining money under false pretenses, I call on you to make complete restitution, or suffer the consequences!" His eyes were severe, through the big glasses. Impressively he tapped the leather-covered arm of the divan. "The car is worthless, absolutely and entirely worthless. Junk, indeed, and nothing else. I was obliged to sell her for such. I received but forty-five dollars for her. Your story, sir, has been heard by witness. Do you wish to settle with me privately, or would you rather have me take the matter into court?"

"I — I guess I'd rather settle, but —"

"Very well, sir. The sum of one hundred and twenty dollars will liquidate your indebtedness."

"But I — I ain't got that much on me!"

"How much have you, sir?"

"Ninety-two, sixty!"

"Very well. I will be reasonable. I will accept ninety dollars in complete settlement of all claims. Otherwise — well, matters must take their course."

Jimmy Dill passed a hand up over his pompadour, then, re-signing himself to the inevitable, pulled out his billfold and paid up. Horn Spectacles very gravely pocketed the money. Then, as the brakes began to grit,; he reached for his suitcase; stood up; and putting on his hat, left the car.

Dill, in a collapse against the cushions, feebly shook his head.

"Can you beat it?" he whispered huskily. "Goodnight! *Can — you — beat — it?*"

IV.

AS THE TRAIN pulled out of the little way station, Horn Spectacles stood gazing after it, with a smile.

"Not too bad, for a casual bit of business," said he contempla-tively. "Ninety beans don't grow on every bush, but a little 'bush' seems to have produced ninety. Some cinch, eh?

"Good idea to carry a full assortment of cards, comprising all the more common names. A man in my line of high-grade confidence specialties never knows when one or the other will come in handy. Now, for instance, if I hadn't just happened to have a card with the name 'Robinson' on it, this flier in junk couldn't have been pulled across, and I'd have been out ninety.

"I wonder who Robinson really was, though, and what hap-pened to Liz?

"I wonder!"

THE SILO

THE ROARING of the eight horse-power gasoline-engine and of the voracious ensilage-cutter, out there in the yard, blending with the windy chatter of the cut corn as it skittered up the pipe and whirled down into the dark silo, masked the coming of Lucky Ruggles. Pownall swung up from broadcasting a shovelful of ensilage that he had dug out of the swiftly growing mound under the pipe, to find himself confronted by the man he feared and hated more than any in this world.

Ruggles grinned, and spat tobacco. An absurd figure to be afraid of — a slouching hobo, with an old cloth cap on, a long black coat possibly stolen from some scarecrow, and torn trousers tucked into a pair of worn out high boots that a farmer's wife had given him. A weak figure, unshaven and watery-eyed; but packed with potential dynamite for Pownall, none the less.

"Hello, there, Powdy!" the hobo greeted the proprietor of the farm. He swaggered a little, with dirty hands deep in trouser pockets, and scuffed his boot-toes into the soft ensilage. "Glad t' see me, ain't you? An' I'm sure glad t' see *you*! This is my lucky mornin'. They're all lucky mornin's to Lucky Ruggles. That's me!"

Pownall could only stare, with fallen jaw. The in-whirling fodder, shot down from the curved pipe high aloft, flicked him with bits of corn-leaf and stalk. At his side, now that he had stopped shoveling, swiftly rose the pile of chopped corn. Only unceasing toil with the shovel and with trampling feet could keep it level in the silo.

"Well, ain't you glad to see an ole friend like me?" demanded Ruggles, squinting with that evil, watery eye. This eye gladdened at sight of his victim's fear. Not even the vague light from the hole in the roof, where the pipe came through, could mask the lines and hues of terror on Pownall's bearded face.

"How — how the devil did *you* git here?" stammered Pownall. He raised the shovel as if to strike.

"Lay off on that rough stuff!" commanded Ruggles, his stubbly jaw stiffening. "You ain't never gonna hit *me*, see?"

"Git outa here!"

"When I'm damn good an' ready! I didn't come here to —"

"You got no right on this here farm. Git!"

Ruggles only laughed.

"You got the nerve, I must say!" he gibed. "After what I'm wise to about you! Now, looka here, mister. I'm gonna have a little privut talk with you, see? We got a few minutes all to our lonesomes. This here's a swell place fer a privut talk, ain't it?" He glanced appraisingly about the silo. "Nobody seen me come. Nobody knows I'm here. So it's all hunky-dory. Some luck, hey?"

"Cut that out!" retorted Pownall. "I got nothin' to say to *you!*"

The men's voices were hardly audible over the droning roar of the machinery, the whirring of the corn. This racket had kept Pownall from hearing Ruggles as the hobo had climbed the ladder into the silo.

Unseen by the workers in the yard, Ruggles had crept up through the meadow, skirted the stone wall and gained the south side of the barn. Here a door had admitted him. The rest had been easy. Now, with that grin of conscious and cruel power, he confronted the gray-faced victim of his blackmail.

"What d'you want o' me?" Pownall demanded.

"Oh, you don't know! Oh, no! My letter — you got it, all right."

"T'hell with your letter, an' you, too!"

"You ain't gonna come across with that thousand?"

"Git out o' here!"

"All right," grinned the tramp with yellowed snags of teeth. "Suits *me!* But I'm goin' right from here to them insurance people. An' they'll slip me a few, fer wisin' 'em up. I'm playin' in luck, either way. Lucky Ruggles, that's me!"

"They won't believe no bum like you!"

"We'll see about that, mister. An' when you're doin' a five-year bit you'll reckon a thousand bucks is pretty small money to be holdin' out on me. A man what'll stay in the big house ruther'n cough up at the rate o' two hundred bucks a year, ain't *much!*"

"I'll say *you* set the fire! I'll —"

"Ta-ta, mister!"

Lucky Ruggles turned to go. Then Pownall struck.

II.

A SHOVEL BLADE may be a murderous weapon in strong hands of hate and terror.

The hobo crumpled forward. He fell, facedown, in the soft ensilage. Immediately a storm of tiny fragments of corn sprayed itself over his motionless body.

Pownall recoiled against the sweeping curve of the silo wall, his eyes white-rimmed with horror. He dropped the shovel. Flat against the wall his calloused fingers extended widely. His back pressed that wall, as if he were trying to push further away from the silent figure.

"Ruggles!" he cried.

No answer. Then Pownall laughed explosively.

It came as a relief after all. Now that the thing, often dreamed, was really done, the farmer felt a vast lightening of his soul's burden. It wasn't hard, was it, to kill a man? Why, an ox required twice as hard a blow! And a man — but was this blackmailing snake a man?

"Damn you!" mouthed Pownall, and stumbled toward the body.

Already it was half hidden by the tornado of ensilage. Pownall understood where his own safety lay, and laughed again. No one had seen the tramp. No one knew. And here, actively at hand, was burial.

He dragged the body, still face-downward, more into the direct line of discharge of the pipe. He stood up and watched the swift drive of the cut fodder over it. Then an idea whipped him to the quick. What *if* somebody had happened to see, to know? That might be possible. Somebody might have been in the barn. Might be there, even now.

Pownall's heart thrashed, sickeningly. An obsession clutched him that somebody really was in the barn. Quivering, he recoiled. He must know!

He stumbled to the tall row of openings that, one above the other, extended up one side of the great cylindrical pit. Through one of these openings — later to be closed by doors, as the silo should fill — he swung himself to the ladder. His legs shook so that he could hardly clamber down. His hands felt putty-like and lax. He dragged himself out to the barn floor. Horribly afraid, he peered up and down.

His terror had him as a dog has a rat, shaking him. But in spite of everything he felt the surge of an immeasurable gladness. Ruggles was dead! Dead, and well punished for all his threats of blackmail, ruin, imprisonment.

"He was a skunk, anyhow," thought the farmer. "I kill skunks on sight. Damned, egg-suckin' skunks! He's only gittin' what was comin' to him!"

Pownall was sick and weak. His mouth felt baked. He swallowed hard. What he wanted was a drink. Water! He walked unsteadily to the faucet that supplied the horse trough near the big barn door. He drew a dipper of water, and gulped it. The water slopped down his neck and chest, wetting his beard, his shirt. That felt good! He smeared his mouth with his hairy hand, and grew calmer.

"It was comin' to him all right," he repeated, and blinked at the October sunshine, golden through the crimsoned maples by the roadside. "Comin' to him!"

What made Pownall's head feel so queer? He wondered dully. For a few minutes he stood there at the door, breathing hard. No one passed along the lonely road. He could hear the engine and the cutter still at work back of the barn; the shouts of a teamster, bringing up still another load of corn from the field. He grinned, crookedly. He couldn't think very straight, but still he realized that he was safe and that Ruggles had only got what was coming to him.

"Lucky Ruggles!" he gulped. "He played it once too often. Out o' luck fer once. Huh!"

It struck him as something of a joke after all. A grim jest. He was laughing a little as he turned back into the barn.

Was there anybody on the barn? Of course not! What an idea, eh? This was a relief. The empty stalls and stanchions peered at him vacantly. The haymows listened. But no human face was visible. In the silo the corn was still rattling down the pipe, whickering on to the pile.

"Only a tramp," thought Pownall. "Got no home, no folks. I'm a damn fool to worry!"

He breathed deep, and returned to the silo. He felt so glad! Glad it was all over and done with. Glad he was free at last.

"An' it was comin' to him all right!"

He approached the ladder, up along the staring row of openings into the silo. The four lowest openings were closed by doors, each two feet high. That meant eight feet of corn already lay in the silo. He squinted up the ladder, past the haymow, to the roof, where the pipe came through.

"That's great stuff, that corn," he realized. "It'll bury him in no time. Gosh, but this is lucky fer me!"

He felt calm now. The first nervous shock had passed. A great coolness was possessing him. What danger could there possibly be? No one had seen, no one knew. And already the body would be hidden. Even without packing down, the avalanche of corn would bury it. Was there ever such wondrous fortune?

He remained there at the foot of the ladder, thinking. There was no hurry. Let the corn pile in, more and more! The hobo's threats of a year's standing pictured themselves with what vivid detail! How distinctly Pownall remembered that July night on the other farm, the old Marshfield farm! A year ago? More. Fifteen months!

"That place was no good anyhow," said Pownall, and bit tobacco from his plug. Yes, a chew would do him good. He never remembered tobacco tasting so fine.

The old farm had been isolated, played out, unproductive. A losing proposition. Even his housekeeper — old, crabbed Mrs. Green — had not wanted to stay there. He had so longed for a fire, for his insurance money, so that he could get away and buy a place elsewhere! And then that night when Mrs. Green had been gone — that high wind, and the crashing thunderstorm at eleven o'clock. The lightning had struck an elm, close to the barn. Half stunned, Pownall had blinked from the house, out into the deluged dark, the flashing dazzle.

God! Why hadn't that lightning struck the barn?

The thought had flamed into inspiration, whiter than the lightning. A match had done the rest. But the tramp in the haymow had seen. Had understood. Only fifty dollars had shut the tramp's mouth and had got him away into the night before the old hand-tub had come pelting up from the village, dragged by long lines of drenched, panting men in disarray. Strange sights in the blinding glare of the flame-sheets from the barn. Pownall could still hear the lowing of the terrified cattle he had released. Gould still hear the *thud-thud-thud* of the pump-bars.

Nothing had availed. The house connected with the barn by a

low shed had gone, too. Pownall had toiled, sweating and rain-soaked, with the others. He had labored to exhaustion at the pump-bars. No use! The well, sucked dry by the old leathern hose, had made no impression on the howling flames, storm-driven, that had reddened the whole countryside. The house and barn had gone flat in an hour. No one had suspected anything.

Everybody had been kind. Had commiserated him. Later the insurance company had paid to the last penny, without question. For the policy had covered lightning.

Three thousand dollars. Cash. In place of that useless old set of buildings. Then he had sold the land for eight hundred. He had bought this newer, better farm. He had prospered there.

At first he had been afraid. But in a year, in fifteen months, fear had died. Nothing had remained of it but a few words. The words spoken by the hobo as he had slouched away with the fifty dollars toward the blackness of the wood lot:

"Mum's the word fer now! But if I need kale, I'll write. My name's Ruggles. Lucky Ruggles. You'll mebbe hear from me ag'in. An' if you do, you'll be nice to me, won't you? An' shoot me a few bucks? I'll say you will! S'-long!"

For a whole year, no word of the hobo. Maybe, Pownall had hoped, he had got into jail somewhere, or been killed by a freight. So Pownall had ceased to be afraid. Then the scrawled letter had come, demanding a thousand. Pownall had not answered, but his soul had wilted with the blight of a very great fear. And the hobo had come back, just a few minutes ago. And now —

Now the man he had so cringed from, in terror, was lying dead in the silo. And no one know.

"God!" exclaimed Pownall. "Ain't that great, though?"

He climbed the ladder; and as he climbed panic struck him again. That shovel! It might have blood on it. Somebody might have climbed into the silo while he had been getting a drink, and might have found it. Might have found the body, too. His mind leaped to those possibilities. He knew that no one had entered the barn, and yet —

His hands shook as he scrambled up the ladder and sprawled into the gloomy damp of the silo. The little doorway into the silo was green. A kind of subconscious vision touched his mind of another little green door. The door of the room where the electric chair was waiting. With a dry throat and hot pulses the farmer stumbled into the soft masses of the chopped corn, not now evenly spread or trampled down.

His relief was immediate, vast. Nobody was there. The shovel still remained just where he had left it, against the curving silo wall. Its blade was already buried deep in the drift of flicking ensilage. The pipe, far aloft, was still whirling corn with a roar and rattle, in stinging blasts. A heap, five or six feet high, now filled the center of the silo. The heap slanted down on all sides to the level of the corn at the walls. This level itself was about eight feet from the cement bottom of the silo.

"God!" grunted Pownall again, and rubbed his palms up and down along his dirty overalls, as if cleansing them of something. Blood, perhaps. But there was no blood on his hands. Nor on the shovel blade either. It looked quite clean and bright.

Pownall was not an imaginative man. He was a hard-fisted, cold-livered New England farmer. He set to work now, once more spreading and trampling down the corn. At his third thrust of the shovel, he encountered something hard. He prodded, poked away the corn, and saw a boot-heel. He laughed then and fell to his task with a good heart.

Quite as if nothing had happened he labored. With sweat and a great joy, he completed the burial of Lucky Ruggles. Pownall was not afraid any more. Not horrified any more. Only glad. Supremely, triumphantly glad!

The feeling of the corn under his feet, under his shovel — green grave, that for long months would hold its inviolable secret till that secret could be well and finally disposed of — afforded him a kind of terrible joy.

He worked without effort, up-borne by calm powers. Sweat streamed down his face and body. He reveled in it as in the roar of the engine, the clatter of the ensilage in the pipe, the cascading flood of corn still shooting down.

As the silo filled, he closed another door. Later, still another. Soon, four feet of packed corn, neatly on a level, lay above the body of the hobo. By noon this had increased to eight feet and more.

The noon whistle, shrilling far from the village sawmill, shut down the corn-cutting and brought the laboring teams and men to rest. Still Pownall worked on, leveling, stamping down, oblivious to the cessation of the floods of corn. His work seemed to have become mechanical, involuntary. His hands and feet toiled, but his brain took no cognizance of that toil. It was busied with the greatest happiness that it had ever known.

When the man from the engine came into the barn to see what progress had been made in filling the silo, and clambered up the ladder, he found Pownall still shoveling, still tramping the corn. This was now sixteen feet above the cement bottom.

"Hey, there!" the engine man laughed, elbows on the bottom of the door into the silo. "What's the matter o' you, anyhow? Time to quit. Fine mornin's work!"

Pownall started, seemed to waken as from a dream.

"You betcha!" he answered, leaning on his shovel. "We'll pack this to the roof by night. A fine morning's work is right. The best *I* ever done!"

III.

OVER AND OVER, all that autumn and half the winter, Pownall calculated everything to a nicety. He did not brood with any regrets, any compunction over the killing. Insensitive, conscienceless, he lost no sleep. But many of his waking hours were devoted to the approaching last chapter of the story. No detail was overlooked.

"He'll keep fine," thought the farmer with exultation. An enduring happiness was his now that the sole witness to his arson and his insurance fraud had vanished. "He'll keep, same as ensilage keeps, in the middle o' the silo. There's tons o' corn on him, an' it's reekin' with alcohol." The alcohol had, indeed, been so plentiful in this corn that some of it had even run out at the bottom of the silo. "He's pickled, that's what he is. He'll be in good shape when I git down to diggin' him out. But I got to be ready fer that, too."

He planned everything to a T. There had been thirty-six feet of corn in the silo, covering eighteen doors up the side. Seventeen cows would eat about three-quarters of the ensilage in four months. The body of Ruggles lay about eight feet from the bottom of the silo. Thus, in the natural course of events, Pownall would exhume the body about the middle of February.

"But I ain't goin' to wait exactly fer that," decided Pownall. "By February fust I'll git him out, an' plant him. That'll be the safest way."

He arranged every detail, even to having his housekeeper, Mrs. Green, plan on a visit to her married daughter in Haverhill, about that time. He thought even of the blanket he intended to take with him into the silo, to wrap and carry the body in. Nor did he forget that he would dig the grave in the barn cellar, and then install a pigpen over it.

"There ain't no possible way fer a slipup," said he to his soul. "This here farm is 'way off the main road. Nobody much comes by here but the R. F. D. man; an' of a Sunday *he* don't come. With the barn door shet, an' workin' early of a Sunday mornin', it'll go through. Sure as death an' taxes!

"In the books they allus gits ketched. But I won't git ketched. Nobody knows he was here. He ain't got no folks, ner nothin'. There *couldn't* be nothin' safer!"

He carried out his plans with the cold accuracy of a machine. On Friday, February 2, Mrs. Green departed for Haverhill. She left him a pantry full of cooked victuals and an infinitude of directions about household details. When he had driven her to the desolate railroad station and had seen her depart, he returned home, ready for his task. The frozen solitude of the farm did not appall him. It only cheered him with assurances of complete and final success.

That afternoon he built a pigpen in a dry corner of the barn cellar. So far, so good. He slept well that night. Next day, Saturday, he dug a deep, ample grave in the pigpen. Again he slept well. Things were going forward, eh?

Sunday his alarm clock awoke him very early. His nerves were steady as a church, ready for the *finis* of his book.

He fortified himself with a hearty breakfast and two cups of hot coffee. By lantern-light he went out to the barn, where the blanket was already waiting. A crisp winter morning, long before dawn. Hard stars and a steely, gibbous moon surveyed him as his alert form crossed the yard. His boots creaked the frozen snow.

He foddered and grained the cattle, watered them, and milked, all as usual. Then he tossed the blanket into the silo, climbed up there with his lantern, took his fork and began digging.

The lantern hung on a nail driven into the silo wall, betrayed no anxiety on his bearded face. What anxiety could he feel? So far, all his actions had been quite natural, without suspicion. He reckoned that it would take him only an hour to exhume and carry the body into the cellar, bury it and turn the pigs into the new pen. His chances of discovery were, practically speaking, just *nil*. Not once had anybody called at the farm so early. No one would call this particular morning.

"Dead easy!" he grunted as he dug.

Pownall was in no sense an emotional man, nor was he given to introspection. The job ahead of him did not even strike him as particularly unpleasant. It was just something that had to be gone through with as efficiently and expeditiously as possible.

The empty silo doors, ranged in a vertical tier, gave him his exact location. Twelve of these doors were now visible. That meant twenty-four feet of the corn had been used. Counting up from the cement floor of the silo, he knew the body lay opposite the top of the fourth door, or about eight feet from the bottom. Pownall had reviewed this fact unnumbered times, and felt as positive of it as of life itself. There could be no slightest question about it. Pownall would have gambled his existence on the fact that Ruggles was about four feet below the present level of the ensilage.

Digging down four feet into a tightly packed mass of fine-cut corn is a fairish job, but not formidable.

"I'll have him out o' here, an' buried, inside of an hour," Pownall assured himself. He spat on his hands and fell vigorously to work.

Steadily, unemotionally he toiled, his breath steamy on the chill air. His shadow, huge, grotesquely distorted, rose and fell as the smoky lantern — specially filled for the occasion — cast it against the opposite wall. Above a huge black vault peered down at him from the snow-covered, conical roof.

Only familiar sounds came to him from the barn — the lowing of a cow, the trampling of a horse. Outside, silence. And inside the dim wooden cylinder, silence, too; silence, save for the deep breathing of the farmer, or an occasional *thud* as a forkful of ensilage struck the wooden wall.

Pownall labored for perhaps twenty minutes, in the remembered spot where he had seen the cascades of fresh ensilage — now brown and reeking of fermentation — whirl down on Lucky Ruggles, burying him. In spite of the February cold, sweat began to runnel his face and trickle down his beard. He stopped now and then to smear it off, and spit. Resting on his fork, which he plunged into the corn, he eased his back and recovered his wind.

"I'm 'most down to him now," he reckoned. "Cal'lated to of found him afore, if I'd knowed where to look exactly. But I'll git him now, in a few minutes."

He still felt calm enough, though his heart was beginning to trip a little. After all, he'd rather be working at something else. But — well, it had to be gone through with, hadn't it?

Again he dug.

"Ha!" he grunted with a leap of the heart. "There's a boot now!"

He stooped and tugged at the boot. He pulled hard. There was no resistance. The boot came right up, free, in his hand. He all but tumbled backward.

"*Huh!* That's funny!"

Furiously he shoveled, breathing hard. Another boot — also empty.

"Lord! What —"

He remained there, peering down at something he could not understand.

He stumbled over to the lantern, his face gray. He unhooked the lantern, carried it to the trench he had dug in the ensilage. Its smoky red gleam revealed the terror on his face. Panting, now, with sweat clabbering on his forehead, he swung the lantern down into the vacancy of the empty trench.

"Jest two boots, an' that's all!" he mouthed. "But — God — it can't be so! It can't! He was here an' I killed him. An' buried him. A dead man can't git out of his boots an' dig through tons o' fodder, an' git away! He can't. He can't!"

Pownall hung up the lantern again with sick hands. He hurled the boots to one side. Half blind with horror that could not reason, he flung himself once more into his labor.

As he dug he wheezed. Disjointed words came gulping from his throat, a throat constricted as by a cold and lifeless hand:

"A dead man can't — he can't — he can't —"

They found him, late that night, still digging.

The mooing and trampling of the untended cattle brought a couple of passing neighbors into the barn. A gleam of light from the silo, and the sound of laughter, drew them thither.

A great mound of ensilage had been tossed out, on to the barn floor. Tons of it. They climbed this, to the open door, and peered in.

Below their level, they looked down on the madly toiling figure of a man who dug aimlessly, tossing the fodder back and forth, sifting it, sometimes even scraping to the very bottom of the silo. This man dug, staggered, laughed, wept, dug again, and called with horrible blasphemies on the name of God to witness that a dead man cannot move.

By the smoldering rays of the expiring lantern the sight appalled them.

"Hey, Pownall! Hey, you, Pownall!" shouted the bolder of the two neighbors. "Whatcha doin'? What's the matter o' you?"

Pownall answered nothing. It seemed as if he could not even hear them. Haggard, with sweat-blinded and ghastly face, he labored aimlessly. A creature wounded to the death, a mole that perishes even as it digs, he groveled in the corn. He flung himself on hands and knees, shoved his arms into the fodder, pawed and clutched and cursed, prayed, laughed again. The laughter was worst of all. That froze the neighbor's blood.

Suddenly the lantern shot a sick flame up, quivered and went out. Utter dark fell in the silo. Through the dark the curses and laughter echoed.

The men recoiled, horror-stricken. Clinging to each other, they stumbled down the pile of ensilage, and to the door. To the blessed freedom of the wintry night.

"Gawd A'mighty!" quavered one, his face twitching. "He's went plumb crazy! Run fer Dr. Abbott!"

"I — I dassen't go alone, Ed! You come, too!"

Thus quaking to the roots of their souls they ran through the snow for help. And as they ran a horrible voice echoed dully through the blackness of the silo of the barn:

"I got him, anyhow! He's *somewheres* here — if I — could only find him. A dead man can't — he can't — *can't* —"

IV.

THE OLD NEWSPAPER, wrapped round the "hand-out" that a good wife had given the hobo at a Connecticut back door, furnished that knight of the road a few minutes' literary diversion.

Seated by a little fire of chips alongside the railroad, in the afternoon sunshine of late April, he read the paper as he leisurely devoured the good wife's meat and bread.

All at once he grinned, with narrowing eyes that watered rheumily.

"Well, by the livin' jing!" he grunted. "That must be him! John W. Pownall — that is him!"

With keenest interest and enjoyment he reread the article, then glanced at the dateline of the paper.

"Two months ago, huh? An' nutty! An' in the nut-foundry at East Bridgewater, incurable! I allus thought the squirrels'd git him if he didn't watch out!"

Ruminatively, the hobo pondered. He swallowed the last of his snack, wiped his unshaven lips on his sleeve, and produced part of a cigarette from a formless pocket of his black coat. He lit the cigarette with a blazing chip, and inhaled smoke. His mind worked but slowly. He was conscious now of mingled pain and pleasure.

"There goes all my show of ever gittin' that thousand," he cogitated. "But I'm even with him fer this, anyhow." He rubbed an ugly scar on his thick skull.

"That was some wallop, believe me! Almost knocked me out. Lucky fer me I had sense enough fer to lay still an' do the 'possum act. What?"

He smoked out the fag, and tossed it into the fire, then laughed with ugly tusks.

"Nutty!" said he. "Sure, he's nutty now, an' he must o' been then. A guy what'd bean a feller just fer asking fer a thousand must o' been plumb bugs.

"Gee! I got out of it easy, I'm thinkin'. If he hadn't of went outa that there silo, an' gave me a chanst t' slip off me boots an' pussy-foot it up that ladder inta that haymow, an' lay there all day till I could make my getaway that night, God — he sure might o' bumped me off!

"Lucky, I calls it. Lucky! Lucky Ruggles, that's *me*!"

FIRE FIGHT FIRE

Hᴀʀᴅʟʏ ʜᴀᴅ ᴅʀ. ᴅᴇᴀɴᴇ Miller landed at the Dorian Club's boathouse to take on more supplies for the rest of his hunting-trip, when Merle, the pop-eyed negro boy, thrust into his hand a telegram marked *Rush*.

Dr. Miller ripped open the envelope with a large, well-tanned forefinger, and this message flashed into his brain;

> Come at once; stop for nothing; urgent operation; must have you. Benedict.

The doctor pursed his lips into a "Whee-e-ew!" of annoyed surprise, and shoved back his canvas hunting cap. His curly hair — he hated it — lay heavily clustered on his forehead; his eyes ached with the sunlight and the glare of the Lower Bay; he was dog-tired all over. Decidedly this message did not please him. He turned it over meditatively, as if he might find on the other side some solution to the difficulties of a twenty-mile train-ride and a delicate operation at the other end, without even so much as a change of raiment; but the blank yellow paper offered him no counsel.

"Hang this!" he grumbled, striking the paper with his big left hand. "Hang it! Can't a fellow clear out for a couple of weeks to shoot ducks and try to forget a girl" — he groaned at certain memories — "without this sort of thing yanking him back to work again? If I was what she called me — a coward — I'd fake up some excuse, or say I never got the message; Merle, here, isn't above money and without price — but no, guess I'll have to cut for town."

Out came his watch. Twelve minutes to train-time — no, the electrics couldn't possibly do it.

"Here, Merle, you blackbird!" he commanded, weighing a half-dollar suggestively in his broad palm. "You bring me a telegraph-blank and rustle me up a cab the quickest you ever did in your life! While it's coming, fix me a basket with sandwiches and a bottle of —

no, I can't even have that if I'm to operate! Well, make it, Pollinaris! Scoot, now, you calcined charcoal!"

II.

DR. MILLER'S ENTRANCE into the operating room of the Trail Hospital, clad in full khaki hunting-togs, with even his revolver and cartridges girded around his equator like the rings of Saturn, caused a flutter of consternation among the three prim nurses waiting beside the little glass and iron table. The Trail Hospital, private, sedate, conservative, maintained its dignity even in the face of life and death emergencies. Dr. Miller was, at times, a disturbing factor in its routine, though an absolutely indispensable one. The three nurses, not having been informed regarding the situation, exchanged scandalized glances.

"Where's Benedict?" demanded Miller curtly of Miss Willett, quelling the young women with a sweep of his eye — an eye which never yet had been disobeyed.

"Hullo, there, doctor!" answered a voice from the sterilizing-room. "I'm washing up. Say, but I'm glad you're here, though! Come on and scrub."

Miller strode through the door.

"What's the trouble?" he asked.

"Trouble enough — patient's just being etherized now. I was never so relieved in all my life as when I got your wire saying you'd be here. Everything's figured out to a T. If you'd been late, though —"

Benedict looked around with a grimace as he soused his hands in the third solution, preparatory to drying them on a sterilized towel.

"Who is it? What is it?" Miller persisted, the while he slipped his operating-tunic over his coat and took a handful of green soap. He glanced sharply at the younger man, his classmate of five years ago, now his assistant at the Trail.

"Young woman, about twenty-five or so," answered Benedict. "Didn't get the name very well, but I think she's from Hillingdon. No matter — she's a stranger here, anyway."

"Well, what's the difficulty?" interrogated Miller, a shade of impatience rising in his voice. The word "Hillingdon" recalled the bitter quarrel, the shame of being misunderstood, the curt dismissal — all the miserable affair which his hunting-trip had so signally failed to obliterate. "Well, what is it?"

"Aneurysm of the left jugular."

"So?"

"Yes — rather unusual, eh?"

"I should say so. Badly distended?"

"Liable to end fatally any hour — been coming on for some time, but diagnosed as neuralgia or some such foolishness — very unfortunate error of some local doctor down there."

"Why didn't you call in Ferrell, or go ahead with it yourself?"

Benedict shook his head.

"No, no," he answered, "I thought we'd better wait for you. Don't want to throw bouquets, you know, but —"

"There now, that'll do!" grumbled Miller, rinsing his hands. Miller was impervious to compliments. Not even the fact that at twenty-nine, only four years out of college, he was already something of an authority on aneurisms could upset his strictly impersonal attitude toward his own skill. "Everything all ready?" he went on. "Hemostats? Scalpels? Silver wire? Must have it very fine, you know — can't wrap a jugular with ship's cable!"

"You'll find everything correct," Benedict assured him. "There, she's being brought in now!"

The quiet opening of a door and the roll of rubber-tired wheels, joined with a sickish whiff of ether, heralded the introduction of the patient into the bright glare of the operating room. Miller heard a whispering and a shuffle of feet as the orderly and nurses laid the woman on the table; then a slight scraping noise told that they were dragging the instrument-stands into position. Benedict walked out to take his place; Miller gave his hands a last dip, a final drying, and followed him.

For a moment he did not see the face of the woman; then Miss Willett drew from it the sterilized cloth, and — Miller's heart gave a sick jump; all the blood in him seemed rushing to it, leaving his ruddy face as gray as winter's dawn. His stout knees trembled; and that steady hand of his, which had so often held the even balance between life and death — where was now its cunning? Little glistening diamonds of sweat came prickling out all over his forehead.

He stepped back into the sterilizing-room, shaking like a frightened child.

"Oh, Lord!" he gasped. "*You* — Isabelle! Benedict," he called a moment later, in a choking voice, "come out here!"

The assistant surgeon came to him.

"Say, Benedict, I — I —" stammered Miller. "Say, what does this mean? How did Isa — she — this patient get here? She — she — why —" He choked, stared, remained speechless.

"What in time's the matter with you?" questioned Benedict, alarmed. "Touch of sun?"

"No — nothing! Just tell me the — the circumstances, can't you?"

"Why, there's nothing much to tell. Got a telephone from Mrs. Dill, up there on Benton Avenue, you know, last night. Went up. Found she had a friend visiting from Hillingdon — this woman here. Pain in throat, abnormal pulsation, and all that sort of thing — made the examination — found the aneurysm, that's all. Had her kept quiet till this morning — then brought here. Consultation. Decided to wire you on the chance — you said you'd be at the Dorian today. Well, you're here, and so's the patient — everything all right so far. Get it? Anything outof order? . . ."

"No, no, but —"

"But what? Here's your patient all anesthetized and waiting. It's up to you now. If there's any irregularity anywhere, let it go till later. Professional etiquette — if that's it — can't stand in the way now! What's up, eh? You look like a cadaver, and that's a fact! Pull up, Miller, and come along out here!"

The assistant seemed to have taken control; Miller was, for a moment, as clay in his hands. But only for a moment; then he elbowed Benedict out through the door.

"All right," he said. "Get everything ready; I'll be there in a minute." He gripped his strong, sterile hands together so tight that the knuckles whitened under the tan; he clinched his teeth till the big jaw-muscles bunched like cordage. "Now, boy!"

* * *

III.

Dr. Miller's hand was steel and his eyes were as glass when he made the primary incision. His voice was even and low:

"Clip, here — now the scalpel — no, no, the other one — forceps — hold here — so — that's right!"

He was beginning one of the most curious, difficult, and dangerous operations known to surgery — that of exposing and wrapping with silver wire a weakened, swollen artery of vital importance. "Aneurysm" is a word of dread; if one bursts, or if the surgeon's knife slips, cutting the distended walls — farewell!

Miller's knife did not slip; his hand, large and strong, held the keen scalpel with a fine precision of which an etcher might be jealous. His eyes did not wander higher than the patient's throat; all sense of her personality was gulfed in that almost mechanical accuracy, that nerveless, deliberate skill which from the beginning of his career had marked him as one of the few. His face, nevertheless, continued to be putty-gray, and the little diamonds on his forehead did not evaporate.

Benedict seconded him like the able assistant he was; Miss Willett stood at the head of the table, ether-cone in hand; the other two passed instruments, took them from their glass trays of solution, dropped them back, when used, into other solutions. Quiet brooded beneath the glare from the broad skylight — quiet except for the deep breathing of the patient, the clink of the instruments in their trays, or the cool words of the surgeon. The artery lay exposed.

"Now the wire!" commanded Miller; and Miss Schwenk, the second nurse, reached it to him with silver forceps.

"*Brrrrrrrrrrrrr!*"

Through the hospital thrilled and vibrated a harsh electric gong, the gong that meant only one emergency — fire!

Benedict started nervously; the nurses shifted positions a trifle. Miller knitted his broad brows, but otherwise paid no more heed to the strident alarm than if it had been a summons to dinner. He looped the first strand of silver, dexterously introduced the second, then said impersonally:

"Lock the door, please, Miss Schwenk. Lock both doors!"

The nurse hesitated. Through the reek of ether an acrid odor of smoke had filtered into the windowless room; and over the skylight there was drawing something like a bluish veil. Far down the street jangled a faint distant clangor of bells, mingled with a thin wail of fire-engine whistles.

"Lock — the — doors!" repeated Miller, and this time his eyes were on Miss Schwenk.

She gave a nervous little giggle, quite unprofessionally feminine, and obeyed.

"Now bring me the keys," murmured the surgeon, bending to his work. "Lay them right here, please."

His glance indicated a little clear space on the operating-table. Miss Schwenk obeyed again.

"Thank you," said Miller courteously.

The operation continued, Miller icy-cool, the others beginning to fidget a trifle. The engines were drawing near; cries, shouts, hoarse bawlings sounded outside; they heard the clang of the chief's wagon hurtling down the street; the clattering hoofs, the thundering wheels, as the great machines whirled on. A crowd was gathering — the noise welled up as the tide wells against a cliff-shore.

Someone rattled the handle of the operating room door, screeched "Out! Out! East wing's goin' fast!" and then rushed off down the corridor, where immense chaos reigned — whence came cries, groans, the sound of hurrying feet, screams of terror, as nurses and orderlies rushed the patients unceremoniously, in wheelchairs or in their arms, over into the west wing, to temporary safety.

Then, over all that tumult from within and without, blared the hoarse whistle of the heating-plant — three long, bellowing blasts as from a brazen, tortured Minotaur — the signal of extreme-emergency — *"All out!"* And at that sound the tumult waxed into a hurricane of rushing terror.

"Quiet, Miss Chase!" commanded Miller. "Ten minutes, and this patient can be moved — not before! Please sterilize this clamp!"

Calmly he made another loop with the silver wire. Thicker and thicker the smoke puffed in around the door which communicated with the corridor; across the skylight whirled a darkening veil. Miss Schwenk began to sob hysterically.

"Quiet! Quiet!" repeated the surgeon; but Benedict, pale to the lips, interrupted him:

"Really, Miller, this is —"

"Shh-h-h! Hold that hemostat!"

"But — but — five of *us* — we'll be cut off in —"

"Remember you're a surgeon!" was Miller's only answer, yet it covered Benedict's drawn face with a hot flush.

Outside, the engines were whirring and puffing; the tumult was that of a great concourse. Inside, the operating room door was beginning to smoke; the air was thick and blue, difficult to breathe. The skylight was obscured; burning brands and cinders were whirling down upon it, faster and faster. It was growing dark.

"Miss Chase, the lights, please!" commanded Miller.

The wires, he knew, came in from the front, and were as yet intact. As Miss Chase clicked the switch-button, a bright, warm radiance filled the white-walled room. A louder shouting rose outside. The crowd, mistaking the glow from the skylight for the glare of fire, believed the operating-pavilion itself invaded.

Miller glanced up for an instant with contracted brows. "You can go now," said he to the women. "Benedict and I can finish this alone. Get out as quick as you can, and shut the door after you, *tight*! Down the basement stairs and out through the laundry. Understand?"

Two of the nurses, with scared but grateful glances, took unceremonious leave. The key grated; footsteps pattered out through the sterilizing-room — then came a gush of smoke as the corridor door opened and closed. The iron stairs into the basement faintly echoed their running steps — they were gone.

"Well?" asked Miller, looking up and seeing Miss Willett still at the patient's head.

"I'll stay!" said she. "The pavilion won't cave in for five minutes yet, I'm sure — maybe more. I won't desert! Go on!"

She spoke rapidly, with the fever of a gambling chance in her eyes — eyes with dilated pupils and dark, inscrutable depths, that rested upon Miller with a look which no son of Adam ever misunderstands. Miller did not misunderstand — he simply did not care.

"Oh, very well, as you like," he answered. "But go any time you please; nothing but the dressings to do now."

"In that case," spoke up Benedict, "I'm going! You and she can finish all right — this place is afire now — it'll cave in any minute! Look at that door — burning! I'm off!"

He laid down the hemostat he was holding, stood up, and faced Miller defiantly, his face twitching, his eyes glittering in the electric, glare; all around him curled and eddied the thickening smoke.

"Sit down!" said Miller. "Don't be a coward!" His firm hands made the last loop. "Don't let any one ever call you that. It hurts; I know! Hand me over those dressings now, and sit down!"

Benedict, with an oath, started for the door. As he came around the end of the operating-table, Miller, holding his needle in his left hand, flung back his tunic with the right and whipped out his long-nosed revolver.

"You sit down!" said he. "I've got some fire of my own, right here, and it's quicker than what's outside, too! Take your choice — but remember I can't miss at such short range! There, that's right, I knew you'd be reasonable. Hand that tray of bichloride over here — I've got to sterilize my fingers. That gun's aseptic."

He dabbled his hand in the sublimate, carefully dried it on the sterile sheet, and started on the dressings. Benedict crouched in his chair beside the table, dazed, mechanical, obeying as a whipped dog obeys. Miss Willett, breathing hard, helped apply the collodion, the cotton, and the bandages.

The task was nearly done — the blazing corridor door was warping inward; thin little tongues of lire licked up along the panels. Outside reigned pandemonium as the fire spread — spread toward the west wing, unheeding the engines, which shook and sobbed and spat glowing cinders up into the smoky pall. The skylight, all drifted over with firebrands, was sagging, fusing; the air inside the operating room seemed glowing like a furnace, in the electric glare. Then something shook and gave; a roar burst up into the sky; through the fire-shot smoke flared a glorious fan of radiance, and the multitude shouted hoarsely — the east wing had fallen in like a cardboard-house, and the brick operating-pavilion, with blazing roof and cracking walls, was standing alone in that carnival of flame.

"Hose, here hose!" the shout rang. *"Crash!"* went the skylight as a stream hit it; down jingled and clattered a shower of glass, down soused a torrent of muddy water. Miller's big arms and body shielded the woman's face; smoke poured in, down, all about them — gray, greasy, strangling smoke.

"That blanket! That blanket!" cried Miller in a choking gasp.

"There! Now, raise the shoulders! That's right! Now under — now over — so! . . . ."

The woman lay wrapped, head and all, like a monster cocoon.

Smash! smash! The door from the etherizing-room trembles, breaks, gives — sharp spurs of firemen's axes splinter it, shatter the lock — the door breaks down — two, three firemen stumble in, heads muffled, axes in gloved hands.

"Out! Out!" they roar dully. "Only chance is through de winder out here in de nex' room! *Clear out!*"

One seizes Miss Willett and carries her off bodily through the curling smoke. Benedict, shielding his head with his hands, rushes out wildly. Then comes a sudden dash of waters all over Miller and the woman, as some other firemen get a line of hose up the ladder into the next room.

"Wait! Hold on!" yells Miller. "Turn that the other way!"

And gathering up in his strong arms, as if she had been a child, the unconscious woman who had branded him a coward, he bears her out of the now fiercely flaming place, through the window of the etherizing-room, down the swaying, smoking ladder.

SPEED LIMIT

"SHE'S CERTAINLY a jim-slicker!" murmured Judge Amos Bartlett, shifting his quid. He spat accurately, fingered his goatee, and laid a hand on the glossy saddle of the machine.

"By Joe Beeswax! a right smart contraption, ain't she, now that I kin see her by daylight? Looks twice as hun'some as she did last night, when she come. Gosh, I cal'late she wun't take nubbody's dust! Bet two fingers on the choppin'-block, an' resk it, she'll hum!"

With the eye of love he studied his purchase.

Right-o! she surely was a dazzler as she stood there in her bravery of blue and gilt, just uncrated, with the morning sun coruscating her nickel-work.

And, gazing, the old judge felt a thrill of temptation poignant as the long-forgotten passions of a youth now dead these forty years.

"Gosh a'mighty, why not?" he murmured, giving dalliance the rein. "I know I could! I useter navigate a by-cycle as smart as any of 'em; an' the book says this here ain't a mite harder to handle. Dog my cats ef I wanta try her the fust time, with everybody buttin' in an' tellin' me how to break the critter. What I need's a leetle spin all by myself out Pinhook way an' back, jest to git the hang of it like. After that mebbe I wun't s'prise 'em, hey?"

Foreknowing that he would yield to temptation, he still considered a bit.

"Shucks!" he grunted at last "I got any God's amount o' time 'fore court's called. That there Brooks land case ain't docketed till nine. No namable reason I sh'd wait till afternoon. I — I'm a goin' to!"

A new light flashed in the spectacled eye. The judge breathed a trifle faster and spat again.

"I kin!" he exclaimed with emotion. "Reckon I ain't seen my boy Hiram run a wood-cutter an' ensilage-chopper two years fer nawthin'! He allus said it was plumb easy. All ye need's common sense, an' I reckon that's my long shot. I'll take a run right off now, while th' road's clear. Out to Pinhook an' back makes a good route. Jim Hick! I kin an' will!"

Not five minutes higher the August sun had crept when it beheld the judge, there in the barn, communing with the direction book and with the mechanism of the Antelope — consulting them in alternation.

"H-m! Well, that's done now. Tank 'F' is filled with naphthy. Connections at 'B' is all fixed. Leever 'D' is set right. Switch 'X' is turned. Cor-rect!

"'Now,' he read — 'now run the motorcycle along a smooth road a few feet till the ingine begins to explode, then mount, pedal a short distance if necessary, and —' Lawzee! *Ef* that's all they is to it —"

Right glad at heart that his helpmeet, Luella, wasn't visible, he furtively trundled the machine out of the barn, through the straw-littered yard, and out onto the road that led to Pinhook.

"It's jest as well she *ain't* seen me," he muttered. "Women-folks is sech pesky idjits, allus 'skivin' in where they ain't asked ner wanted. Here goes, by gum!"

Back into the toolbox he slapped the half-read book of directions, set the spark, and gave the motorcycle a vigorous push along the road.

At first nothing happened; but all at once, making music to his ears, *put-put! Put! Put! Put-put-put!* the engine caught.

Judge Bartlett made a little rheumatic run, scrambled aboard — though just how he couldn't have told—and, righting the machine that slued hard a lee, Mazeppa was in the saddle!

"Crimus!" he cried as he settled himself firmly, braced his Congress-booted feet on the rests, and gripped the long, curving handles. "The go-darned critter b-b-b-bounces some, d-d-d-don't she?"

But the judge had little time to consider bounces. Already the needle of the speedometer was edging its way past "20," and a sudden wind seemed to have sprung up from nowhere, flailing his long goatee and whiskers as it whipped his wrinkled face.

"G-g-g-gosh!"

All his attention speedily fixed itself on the one problem of keeping the Antelope somewhere in the road. Past him flickered the apple rows of his orchard.

Then the long stone wall that bounded his farm slid away, and right ahead of him yawned the sharp descent of Billings Hill.

The needle now marked 55, and still was rising. With a sickening sensation the judge realized that in his haste to start he had read the instruction book only far enough to learn about starting. The art of stopping he had omitted.

Now some vague, wild notion glimmered through his brain of perhaps trying to get the toolbox open again, find the book, and — but no! Impossible!

He dared not for so much as a single second release the death-grip of even one hand.

To his staring eyes the road had developed into an endless gray ribbon whirling beneath him. Trees, walls, telegraph poles flicked flashing by. The shaking became terrific. Amos felt his store-teeth clatter madly in his gaping jaw.

Crash!

What was it? Only a loose boulder powerless to swerve the force of the great wheels. On sped the machine.

But a twelve-dollar set of "uppers" gyrated through the air, struck the grit far behind, and bounded into the ditch as though in search of the flapping straw hat that but a moment before had sky-hooted rearward in a meteor trail of dust.

The Bean place loomed ahead. Amos glimpsed the huge white barn, the sugar maple grove, the glint of sunlit waters beyond.

"Help! Help!"

The farm lay behind. Vaguely a dog's barking mingled with Ezra Bean's startled shout. The spattering roar of the engine swallowed all.

"Jay Ree-oo! *Team!*"

Delrine Bates reined his ton of hay aside just in time to clear a streaking glint of blue, to which clung a crouching figure — clung with yells, while coattails and whiskers streamed straight behind like gonfalons of woe.

Swerve! Bounce! Slue!

With a sickening yaw to port the Antelope flickered through Pinhook, hazed with dust and hens, and struck the Shag Pond Road — a five-mile circuit, now the judge's only safety.

Dana Cole leaped to the telephone and hurled hot messages broadcast all up and down the farmers' amalgamated lines:

"Ev'body clear th' roads! Teams, youngins, poultry, pigs, keep off! Jedge Bartlett's run away with by a motorcycle! He's lickin' it raound th' lake!"

Thus Amos had a clear track. Hastily all traffic was diverted into barnyards and front doors. Infants and animals were impounded. And fences all along the line began to fringe themselves with an anxious yet a well-pleased populace.

Old Dr. Chase hastily laid out splints, needles, bandages, and chloroform, together with a bottle of Gribbins's Peerless Horse Liniment, the only embrocation in his veterinary stock.

"Reckon mebbe I'll git a job yit!" he murmured, nodding with joyous anticipation.

Thus began the judge's motordrome.

Inside of five minutes, having made the complete circle, he once more leaped through the village. A crowd gathered on the platform of Coffin's general store. Some of the younger bloods on the store platform began to time the judge after the fourth complete circuit. ·

Silas Hennberry, who once had been an assistant track-manager at the South Paris fair, got his stopwatch into action. The fifth round gave a record of 4.28.

Then the betting began, even money that the judge would be making it in 4.25, inside of half an hour.

Old Pop Bicknall offered two to one that the judge would "come up 'mongst the missin'" before the end of the tenth heat. 'Raish Cole took him, and Uncle Sessions held the total stakes of seventy-five cents.

The news spread over the countryside like an oil-film on water. Observation-parties began to coagulate at vantage points. Every impinging road brought in its quota by "rig" or afoot.

The semi-occasional trolley from Milton Plantation to Pinhook began running specials of the entire rolling stock of one car, with record-breaking crowds aboard.

Luella Bartlett, the judge's wife, arrived at the Bean place at 7.32 behind a lathering nag, just in time to catch sight of a vanishing whirl of dust. At this she waved her umbrella, screaming:

"Amos! You, Amos! My soul an' body, Ame! You stop, this 'tarnal minute! Hear me?"

Then she collapsed in hysterics. They had to throw water over her, which they rushed in pails from the horse-trough at the barn.

Meanwhile, other and more serious matters were shaping. For "Deak" Saunders, driving into town behind his goose-necked calico mare, suddenly became aware of serious trouble impending.

Hardly had he struck into the Lake Road when his ruminations about the Brooks land case received a ghastly jolt.

Thus were his pleasant assurances running:

"I got Jeff Brooks where I want him now, by gary! Ef the case is called, an' don't default — an' it's a goin' to be called or I'm a preacher — *ef* it's called, that there mowin' lot's as good as mine a'ready! Oh, I got him fer sure!"

Into these cheerful reflections exploded impending disaster in the shape of a crackling, fire-spitting comet bestridden by a half-glimpsed form that grimly clung and crouched and vanished down the pike.

"Whoa, durn ye!" he exhorted, sawing at the lines. "By the Gre't Deludian! What's *that*?"

Even as faint cheers became audible from the direction of Pinhook, Ronello Bowker came running, waving wild arms.

"Git out o' the road! Clear th' road!" he panted. "Ain't ye heerd?"

"Heerd what?"

"Jedge Bartlett!"

"Huh?"

"He's in a hell of a quand'y! Went an' got himself run away with on a motorcycle, an' —"

"Sho'! Was *that* —"

"Yup! An' fer Heaven's sake, git off'n the road! He'll be raound agin in less'n no time!"

Deak stared and went yellow.

"But — but —" he stammered. "It can't be! He's a goin' to hear that case at nine, an' —"

"Hear nawthin'! *You* hyper!"

Rudely Ronello hauled the mare into Orrington's barnyard.

"Now, ye 'tarnation fool!" he shouted. "You keep off'n the track! Want a wreck, do ye? Ef he hits ye, neither o' you'll last as long as Jed Perkins stayed in heaven."

"Y' mean that's really th' jedge, Ronello?" insisted Deak. "My crimus! How long —"

"He's be'n goin' better part of an hour a'ready. Raound an' raound th' lake. Dassent git off'n that road looks like. His only chanst is to hang right to it till his napthy gins out or suthin' busts on him."

"My land o' livin'! An' ye say he ain't goin' to stop fer court?"

"How in Tunket *kin* he? He's fergot how t' stop her! He'll mebbe keep it up all day — that is, ef he don't peg out fust an' tumble off. Why, what's the matter? You look bluer'n a whetstun!"

Deak Saunders, suddenly vitalized into intense activities, leaped from his buckboard.

"Jeems Rice!" he bellowed. "Ef that 'ar case ain't called I stand t' lose thirty dollars! Quick! Git an auto-mobyle! I'll chase him! I'll holler to him how t' shet her off!"

Ronello snorted.

"Hain't no machine in this caounty kin ketch him!"

Far down the road a distant sound of cheering once more began to float upon the morning air. Then, bursting into the sphere of Deak's consciousness, leaped a crackling roar.

Br-r-r-r-r-r-r! Zip-p-p-p-p-p-p-p!

Once more the comet streaked and vanished.

"By gosh all lightnin'!" execrated Saunders, clinging to the fence and staring with horror-smitten eyes. "That's *my* finish! Thirty —"

He whirled on Ronello.

"Gimme a sheet — brush — paint! I'll make a big sign—tell him how t' shet off th' spark or dreen th' napthy-tank, an'—"

"Sign?"

"Yup! An' hang it 'cross th' road —"

"Idjit! He lost his glasses, teeth, hat an' wig an' every durn thing 't would come off'n him 'fore he'd went raound six times! An' even ef he had his specs, *he* couldn't read no sign, clip he's goin'! Now, you better fergit it an' —"

But Deak heard him not.

Already he had turned and was legging it at full speed through the barnyard toward the lake.

After him stared Ronello.

"Plumb crazed!" he muttered, shaking his head.

Deak, however, was far from crazed.

Even in his seeming madness lay a very definite meaning. At the best gait of his gangling, rawhide-booted legs he racked through the orchard and down to the shores of Shag Pond.

"It ain't more'n half a mile wide here!" he panted, "I kin row over to the icehouse in ten minutes. Say, ef I ever needed t' dig in it's *naow*!"

Mightily he dug in, with Ronello's punt and oars, borrowed sans formalities in the way of asking permission. As never, the waters foamed from that blunt prow; as never, the wake frothed behind.

A reek of sweat under the ardors of the August sun, Deak travailed. Blisters? Weak heart? Asthma? Pooh! The objective of the Chase pasture and the icehouse were lodestones to his fevered soul.

"By gary!" he grunted. "I'll stop him afore he gits killed or thar'll be a dead jedge in these here parts!"

The punt touched mud. Deak leaped through muck and slime, split the cattail jungle, and sprinted across plowed land to the scene of campaign.

Just this side of the big gate into the Chase pasture the Lake Road swerved to the left to clear a broad arm of the pond. This arm, shallow and still, furnished the village ice crop, as the ramshackle building there attested.

Down toward the icehouse ran a road, tangenting off from the main highway which was now functioning as the judge's amphitheater, whereon he was being speeded to make a rural holiday.

To the water this straight, ice-hauling road descended at a passably sharp grade. It terminated in a kind of near-wharf, to which a few boards, though rotten, still adhered.

Heroic as Horatius at the bridge, Deak sprang to the pasture gate.

From its hinges he wrenched it. His strength was as the strength of ten, because —

"*Br-r-r-r-r-r-r-r-r-r-r!*"

A slatch of wind brought for a second a vicious purring to his ears.

"Jumpin' jews-harps! Comin' a'-ready!" he gulped.

Across the road he dragged the heavy gate.

"He either takes th' water or he stops right here!"

Bracing the barrier erect, he stood there with wide and staring eyes, blanched face, white lips, directly in the path of the on-roaring avalanche.

"Br-r-r-r-r-r-r-r-r-r!"

Deak felt very ill, but stood his ground;

Then, a quarter-mile up the road, a clattering rocket leaped over a crest. Instantly it spun the distance down, trailing dust-banners.

Deak, yelling like a maniac, waved one arm and held the gate up with the other.

The rocket took the tangent. Past Deak flicked a streak of blue, flame spitting.

Then, even as Deak dropped the gate and bolted for the wharf, a high-pitched, rising yell was choked in the middle, and a geyser belched.

White water flung aloft in frothing sheaves. These slapped back into the center of wide-spreading circles, where flailed a dazed and frantic object.

Deak dived.

The rest was just a clinching and a dragging.

"Saved yer life, jedge! *Saved yer life!*" rose Deak's voice, triumphant, from the mélée.

Twenty-five minutes later the judge, with dry clothes on him and hot drinks in him, was nigh himself again, in Deak's kitchen. When Mrs. Saunders had dug the mud out of his ears he felt better. After all, he was still alive.

The motorcycle, intact, stood drying against Deak's barn. On the barn floor Deak was harnessing Kit, his other horse, into the Democrat wagon.

A growing crowd gawked along the fence; but Deak was answering no questions. There was still time to get the judge to court, provided no time was frittered in trivialities.

Suddenly Jeff Brooks, the defendant, drove into the yard. His horse showed signs of hard usage. With Jeff was Sheriff Titus. Both men leaped out and advanced toward the barn.

Deak's heart sank. The newcomers looked alarmingly in earnest. But Deak paid no heed. He wanted no speech with them.

They, however, harshly invaded the barn.

"Where's th' jedge?" demanded Brooks.

"What's that to you?"

"Nemmind! Where is he?"

"None o' your damn business! He's my company now. He's all right 'thout none o' your buttin' in, Jeff Brooks!"

"What you hookin' up fer?"

"Well, I reckon I ain't got no call t' inform *you*, but, between you an' me, I'm gittin' ready t' carry him daown to th' courthouse. Any objections?"

Hotly Deak faced the pair. Brooks grinned, eying the harness that depended from Deak's vigorous hand.

"No, I can't say as I've got any real objections t' your hookin' up, as sech," he answered. "Only, it wun't do ye no good. They ain't goin' to be no land case heard, that's all. It's goin' by default, an' I win!"

"No case?" stammered Deak.

"Why not? Who's goin' t' stop me, or *him*?"

"Titus here is, I reckon!"

"Haow? Consarn ye!"

"Do yer duty, officer!" cried Brooks.

"I got a warrant here fer th' jedge's arrest," announced Sheriff Titus. "An' one fer you, too, Deak Saunders."

"A — Why — wha-what fer?" And Deak's jaw dropped.

"You, malicious mischief, destruction o' property, an' obstructin' the public highway. Him —"

"Huh?"

"Him, exceedin' the legal speed limit of ten miles per hour in this here township. An' —"

Just then the assault and battery took place!

The rest was sheer "propaganda of the deed" all over the barn floor, out into the hen-yard, and ending after some fifteen minutes in the far corner of the pigpen.

This new case, of resisting an officer, is still in court, and has been put over till the March term. Much depends on the status of the set of harness as a dangerous weapon.

There is also Deak's counter-suit against Brooks for attempted mayhem. But the fact that Brooks, though he undeniably bit Deak on the right leg and essayed to chew off one thumb, did no material damage because of a total lack of teeth, has a vital bearing on the matter.

It is a complex case.

Judge Bartlett resolutely declines to discuss it.

THE LONGEST
SIDE

"NOW SEE HERE, BOGAN," said Cozzens, when his touring car had struck into the long, smooth, beach boulevard. "You're my confidential right-hand man, and I can talk plainer, perhaps, than I ever have before."

"You can," answered Bogan — "Best-policy" Bogan, by nickname. "Must be somethin' mighty important, or you wouldn't be drivin' yourself, an' you wouldn't of took me out, this way."

"It *is* important," admitted the politician. "And in an important deal, there's no place like an auto. No keyholes for people to listen at in an auto. No chance for dictaphones. Give me an auto for absolute privacy, every time."

"Correct. What's on your mind?"

"You've got to find me a 'fall guy' for that Wheat Exchange Bank forgery and the Hinman murder that grew out of it. A good, high-class fall guy. No roughnecks."

"What's the idea?"

"I might as well speak right out in meeting. I've got to have my daughter Nadine marry Coolidge Brant."

"Assistant district attorney, you mean?"

"Yes," assented Cozzens. "The way things are shaping now, I've just got to have a string on that young man. He's directly in line for the district attorney-ship, inside of two or three years, and I want —"

"I see," smiled Bogan. "Honesty's the best policy, all right. It's a case of rip things wide open, after that, an' get away with it clean, eh?"

"You put it rather crudely."

"Facts is facts. I get you, the first time. An' the daughter's balkin'?"

"I'm afraid she is, a little. She and Brant have been going round together for over a year, but he hasn't made good. That is, not enough to suit her. She's got ideas about efficiency, like lots of girls these days. She won't have him till he's shown some real pep. The press is slamming him, some. So —"

"I'm wise. If he can land somebody right, for those stunts —"

"What I like about you, Bogan," said the politician, "is the way you grab an idea. Well, now, can you work the law of supply and demand for me again? You've done it before. Can you do it once more, and do it strong?"

"Sure! How much is it worth to a man that'll stand for the pinch an' go through?"

"That depends," judged Cozzens, opening the throttle a notch. His big blue car hit a livelier pace down the summer-sunlit boulevard. "Naturally I'm not looking to throw money away. I want you to put this through as cheap as you can."

"Bargain rates won't get a guy to stand a roar for scratch work, knockin' a bank cashier cold, an' bumpin' off a business man. Them's tall, man-size charges to go against."

"I know it, Bogan. But, of course, he won't be running any real risk of anything but a few years in the pen."

"You mean the frame will be fixed so he'll be acquitted on the murder charge, an' will only do time for the forgery an' assault?"

"Yes, and not much time, at that. Four or five years, and then a quiet little pardon, you know. That's at the outside. Maybe he won't draw more than four or five in all. Get me?"

Bogan remained silent, his thin jaws firmly set. He looked out over the bench, the surf, the careless holiday crowd, past which the car was flicking with a *burrrrr* of knobby tires.

"Well?" demanded the politician, "Can you fix it right?"

"Sure. If you'll guarantee the acquittal."

"Oh, *that'll* be O. K."

"Yes, but they never stick a guy with a small charge when there's a big one on him. F'rinstance, if a man's robbin' a hen house, an' croaks a farmer while he's doin' it, you never hear nothin' o' the petty larceny."

"I can fix that, all right. *Got* to, to square the bank. They're sorer than boiled pups, and ready to knife Brant. I'll have him docket it as two separate cases. After the fall guy's cleared of the murder charge, he'll be rearrested on the others and put through."

"I don't see what good that'll do," objected Bogan. "*That*

wouldn't be such a devil of a big feather in Brant's Panama."

"It'll be enough. I'll see that the papers play it up right. Nadine will fall for it strong. She likes Brant, all O.K. It's only that he hasn't done anything much yet. You get the fall guy, Bogan, and I'll attend to my end of it. Well, what say?"

"When do you want him?"

"Right now. And when it comes to cash —"

"I'm on!" smiled Bogan. "I know just the fella."

"Where is he? In town, here?"

"No. New York. An' he's some smooth worker, too, I tell *you*. Show him the coin, an' he'll go the limit."

"That's good enough for me," said Cozzens decisively. "Now well get back to the office and fix you up with expense money to take the night boat down." And Cozzens stepped on the accelerator. "Let's get to it."

"Right!" agreed Bogan. "We'll do this honest an' square. That's always the best policy. Let's go!"

II.

ALBERT VESTINE, Scandinavian by birth, and by profession race-track follower, gambler, and man of various activities — all of them dubious — was wary as a partridge when Bogan called upon him by appointment. Vestine had traveled in too many cities, States, and lands, spoke too many languages, was too clever with his pen and brain, to mistake the type that Bogan represented. Besides, he knew the man personally, which made him all the more cautious.

He received Bogan in his little apartment on Lyon Avenue, the Bronx, and after a few commonplaces such as old-time acquaintances might exchange, asked him his business.

Bogan looked him over before replying. In his own way, Bogan was just as keen as this cosmopolitan with the high-domed forehead, the tendency toward baldness, the thin cheeks of unnatural pallor. As Bogan appraised him, from gray and conscienceless eyes to slim, dexterous fingers, he realized this was, indeed, the kind of man Cozzens needed.

The price Bogan knew would be high. Vestine was no "greasy-coat stiff," to be bought for a song. On the contrary, as Bogan observed his correct linen and cravat, his fine blue suit with the almost invisible vertical stripe, his custom-made shoes, he understood that here was just what the politician had meant when he had demanded: "A good, high-class fall guy. No roughnecks."

He thought, furthermore:

"If I can work this right, there's promotion in it for me, and maybe a little rake-off on the side. I'll play it for a wad o' good, honest graft. Honesty's the best policy, all right."

"Well, Mr. Bogan," inquired Vestine, "what can I do for you?"

"You know me, Al," Bogan replied. "When I say I got a good thing, I got one."

"Yes?"

"An' now, I got a bundle o' kale for you."

"That sounds interesting," smiled the Dane. "Sit down, and tell me all about it." He gestured toward a chair. "How much, why, when, where, and what?"

Bogan sat down, lighted a cigar to give himself countenance — which is one of the principal uses of cigars in this world — and opened up:

"You know the burg I hail from, don't you?"

"Somewhat. I've done a little business there, off and on."

"Well, supposin' some big guy there had to marry his daughter to an assistant district attorney, an' she wouldn't fall for him till he'd pulled some stunt to give him a rep, what would you advise?"

"I'd advise having the stunt pulled, by all means," answered Vestine, likewise sitting down. His eyes were watchful, in his pale, intellectual face.

"Correct," approved Bogan. "We've got to get a fall guy."

"I see. Well?"

"There's hefty coin in the job, an' nothin' more'n about four years — easy years — in the pen."

"What's the case?"

"Some guy forges the name of John C. Wycoff to a check on the Wheat Exchange National, for seven hundred and fifty-five dollars and fifty cents, about three months ago. He's an A-1 scratch man, an' the name looks right. He gets a gents' furnisher named Markwood Hinman to cash it. Hinman's found two days later, croaked, in a hallway on Oregon Avenue. The bull's dope it that Hinman got wise to the scratch work, an' went to see the guy to get him to make good, or somethin', an' the guy bumped him off to keep him from tippin' over the bean pot. That's all old stuff."

"Yes, I remember reading something about it in the papers," agreed Vestine. "The forger cracked Hinman's skull with brass knuckles, didn't he? Back of the left ear?"

"That's the case! Well —"

"What then?"

"The check's in the bank, see? The murder jazzes the bank up, investigatin', an' they get wise the check's a phony. Henry Kitching, the cashier, takes it an' heads for the district attorney's office to raise a roar an' start things. He gets out of his auto on Kent Street an' goes in through the rear alley entrance to the courthouse. He's found slugged there, five minutes later, an' the check's gone. Brass knucks, again."

"Clever!" smiled Vestine. "I suppose the criminal trailed him, and gave him what I believe is called the K. O., from behind."

"Yes, that's the way it looks from here. An' that's how the story'd be put over. But nobody was ever sloughed in for none of it."

"I see. You mean, then, you're looking for a scapegoat in the wilderness?"

"Huh?"

"I mean, a fall guy."

"Oh, sure. Goat, yes — I get you. I see you're wise. Well, then —"

"And this hypothetical goat would have to stand for all the charges, so as to establish the assistant district attorney's reputation for brilliancy?"

"Yes, but the murder charge won't stick, no more'n a red-hot flapjack to a greased griddle."

"How can you guarantee that?" insisted the Dane.

"Cinch!" And Bogan, his eyes kindling with enthusiasm, pulled at his cigar. Vestine, by the way, never smoked, nor did he drink. Both things, he knew, worked on the nerves.

"Please explain?"

"Why, it's this way," Bogan expounded. "We'll fix the story right, an' copper-rivet it, so it can't do more'n establish a strong suspicion. An' it's all circumstantial evidence, too. Nobody *seen* the guy croak Hinman or sneak up on Kitching. That's one point. Another is, we'll have a hand-picked jury. There'll be at least two on that'll stick for acquittal till New York approves of Volstead. So that'll be a disagreement, an' the fall guy gets away with the murder charge, all right. I've been into this thing pretty deep with Cozwith — the man I'm workin' for, an' he'll go through with his end of it."

"Stop beating round the bush, Bogan, I know Cozzens about as well as you do, and I know you're asking me, for him, to take this job, I know, too, he'll go through, if I *do* take it. I've got enough information about him to kill him politically if he tries to renege. You can't double cross, either, or I'd have both of you on a charge of conspiracy to do an illegal act. There are three of us in on this. It's a triangle, understand? All go through, or all collapse! I hope I make myself quite clear?"

"Oh, I get you, all right," answered Bogan, shifting uneasily in his chair. "We'll play this frame-up honest. That's the best policy, every time. All you'll have to go up for will be forgery an' assault."

"H'mmmm! That's enough, I should say," judged the Dane. He pensively brushed a tiny thread from his sleeve with manicured fingers. "How long a sentence —"

"Four years is the limit. Good conduct would cut that down a few months, too. An' you gotta remember this, too — nix on the hard-labor stuff. You got brains, you see, an' —"

"Thank you."

"An' it'll only be a job teachin' arithmetic, or writin' or French an' them guinea languages, in the pen school. See?"

"Nice, pleasant little program you've got all mapped out for me, isn't it?" queried Vestine.

"Sure it is! You can figure you're workin' on salary. So much time, so much coin. Ain't much worse'n bein' a college professor, at that, an' you'll pull down a hell of a lot more coin. We'll have you happy, an' Cozzens happy, an' his daughter, an' Brant, too — he'll think he dug up the case, himself — an' —"

"Regular little love feast, all round, eh?" commented the gambler. "I shall consider myself quite a philanthropist — if I take the job."

"Sure you'll take it!" urged Bogan, with increasing eagerness. This man's quick intelligence and grasp of the situation far exceeded his hopes. Why, things were surely coming very much his way. "You gotta! Think o' the good you'll do! An' ain't it always the best policy to be honest an' do good? You'll square the bank, land a rich wife for Brant, put Cozzens where he can rip things wide open, an' —"

"How about the man that really did the forgery, killed Hinman, and assaulted Kitching?" put in the Dane. "I suppose he'll be happy, too? After I'm tried and acquitted for the killing he'll be safe. And all the time I'm behind bars —"

"Oh, forget him! Just think what you'll be gettin' out of it!"

"I *am* thinking of that, every minute, you can rest assured. And I may as well tell you right now, I'm a high-priced man."

"That's the kind we're after. No cheap stiff, but a ketch that'll really burn some red fire in Brant's front yard! Fine!"

"You realize, of course, it's no joke to be what they call 'mugged,' and finger-printed, and sell four years of my life, and —"

"'Twon't be four. Not over —"

"And then, after it's all over, have to clear out —"

"You've cleared out before now, Vestine, or whatever your name is," asserted Bogan. "Don't play none o' that injured-feelings stuff on me! You got a dozen aliases, an' you're as much at home in China as you are on Broadway. So we'll tie the can to all that 'no-joke' stuff, an' get down to tacks. Will you take the frame?"

"I might, if you pay me my figure."

"Name it!" said Bogan, hands tightening on knees.

III.

"FIFTY THOUSAND dollars, spot cash."

"Oh, hell, no!" Bogan vociferated. "That's ridic'lous!"

"All right, then. *I* didn't ask for the job. You can probably go down on the Bowery and pick up a dozen men that'll do it for a thousand. Don't let me detain you."

"But see here, Vestine —"

"Of course, the fact that after Cozzens gets next to the throne he can clean up a million or two — of course that has no bearing on the case at all. Naturally, such being the prospect, you stick at fifty thousand. That's quite characteristic of men of your stamp. Well, good evening, Mr. Bogan. Don't slam the door as you go out."

"I might go twenty 'thou,' you bein' such a big ketch."

"Rubles, you mean? Bolshevik money?"

"Twenty thousand good hard seeds!"

"Forty," answered the gambler. "That's my rock-bottom."

"Nothin' doin'!" declared Bogan. "Be reasonable, can't you? Make it twenty-five, an' say no more?"

"Twenty-five?" smiled Vestine. "See here, now. I know Cozzens, all right. He's a good sport and likes a fair gamble almost as much as I do myself. I've got a proposition according to his own heart."

"What's that?" demanded Bogan leaning forward.

"Doubles or quits."

"How d'you mean?"

"Double that twenty-five thousand, or not a sou. Fifty thousand or nothing. We'll stick the book for it."

"Gawd!" cried Bogan, and for a moment remained pondering. Into his thin-lidded eyes crept a gleam of craft, exceeding evil. Then he shot back the answer decisive:

"I'll go you!" Much agitated, he stood up.

Calmly, as though about to pitch pennies, instead of gamble for infamy and nearly four years of his life, Vestine reached for a book on the table — *The Arrow of Gold*, for in his literary tastes the Dane was unimpeachable. He laid the book in front of Bogan and handed him a sharp steel paper cutter.

"One stick, each," said he. "Right-hand page, and high last number wins. After you, my clear Alphonse."

Bogan's hand trembled as he made the first cut.

"Two hundred and fifty-one," he spat, with a curse. "*I'm* done!"

"Never say die," laughed Vestine. He took the knife and thrust it deep between the leaves.

"Ninety-one," he announced, without a quiver. He seemed but mildly interested. "Two ones. That's an even break. Come again, Bogan. Here." And he handed back the knife.

"One forty-seven," said Bogan, with an unsteady laugh. "That's a seven-to-ten shot I've got you, or tied. Looks like you're done!"

"If I am, I'll go through just the same," answered the Dane, unmoved. "This is a trifle to some games I've gone against, and I've never welshed yet."

Again he knifed the book. Without the quiver of an eye he flung back the page.

"Eighty-nine," he approved. "That's good. At four years and some months that makes a safe income of about twelve thousand dollars a year. A thousand a month for conducting some little classes in congenial studies — not too bad. And when am I to arrive in your illustrious city, for what you call the pinch?"

Bogan's lips were trembling so that he could hardly answer: "You stay right here, see? That's half the game, lettin' Brant nail you in New York. About ten days from now there'll —"

"And when do I get the excellent and desirable fifty thousand?"

"Oh — let's see — damn it all! Cozzens will raise —"

"That's immaterial to me, my dear Bogan, so long as he raises the fifty — in legal tender, you understand. When is it to be?"

"It's Wednesday, today, ain't it? I'll be back with the stuff Saturday, sure."

"That's perfectly all right for me. Well, then, there's no more to be said. Must you be going so soon?"

"I — I — yes. I better be gettin' along."

"Good night, then. See you Saturday."

"Good night," said Bogan, and departed.

On the stairway he kicked himself, groaning.

"What a damn fool I was not to take him up at forty! Why, Cozzens was countin' on fifty, anyhow. I could of knocked down ten for myself, easy as pie. If I hadn't tried to grab the whole fifty — My Gawd, *when* will I learn that honesty's the best policy, after all?"

IV.

THE WEDDING was one of the most brilliant ever held at St. Simon Stylites Church. Brilliant, too, was the future of Mr. and Mrs. Coolidge Brant held to be. He, as the only son-in-law of so prominent a politician as old Dexter Cozzens; she, as the wife of a man destined in short order to erase the word "assistant" from his present title, received innumerable felicitations.

The papers gave the ceremony brilliant write-ups, and mentioned the brilliancy with which young Brant had run down — from very slight clews — the forger responsible for the death of Markwood Hinman, for the assault on Henry Kitching, and for the theft of the forged check in Kitching's pocket.

The trial, everybody remembered, had been brilliant. Only for the unfortunate "hanging" of the jury, on account of circumstantial evidence, brilliant justice would have been done. The criminal, however — a Norwegian named Aalborg, and rather a brilliant fellow — had got four years. So everybody agreed it had all been very brilliant, especially as the criminal would have remained quite undetected had it not been for young Brant's exceptional legal ability. The general brilliancy made everybody happy, and the papers all predicted a crushing campaign against the crime wave, a cleanup of municipal politics, and all sorts of lovely and desirable reforms.

Not the least brilliant of all developments from the case were those that before very long began to smile down on the stanch old war horse and reformer, Dexter Cozzens. His fortunes soon began to prosper, rapidly though quietly. For brilliancy of this kind is usually kept hidden under bushels — nay, even under pecks. And this, of course, is all as it should be.

Another brilliant feature of the affair, likewise unknown to the public, was the kind of instruction given at the pen by Aalborg, now known only as No. 45327. He undertook to teach the tough idea not, indeed, to shoot, but to explore mathematics, penmanship, and foreign languages. His services were recognized as exceptionally brilliant. They were willing, too. No. 45327 was never "stood out," got all kinds of good-conduct marks, became popular with everybody from the warden down — or up, as you choose — and seemed to enjoy his work almost as if he were getting paid a thousand dollars a month for it. So brilliant a teacher he became, and so model a prisoner, that before long special privileges were extended to him; and, though confined, his punishment hung not too onerously upon his gray-clad shoulders.

Thus everything turned out most brilliantly for all hands, save for Best-policy Bogan. He, strangely enough, took scant joy of anything connected with the matter. For some reason unknown, he seemed to be cherishing a secret sorrow. But as his opinion, one way or the other, was not of the slightest importance, nobody cared.

Thus time passed, Cozzens waxed fat, Brant became powerful.

Aalborg was forgotten by the world; and presently three years and seven months were gone. Then the prison gates swung open for him and he walked out — a man who had well served his purpose, a free man, with his debt to society all paid.

Society, having long since dismissed him from its mind, gave him no slightest heed. What is deader than dead news?

Another question: Does all this mean our story is completely done? Not in the least, as we shall very presently see.

V.

HALF A YEAR after Aalborg's release, Aalborg himself sent in his card to District Attorney Coolidge Brant. The card read: "John Carl Enemark." The visitor requested only a few words in private. Brant, expansive with prosperity and power, bade the clerk usher Mr. Enemark into the private office.

"Mr. Brant," said the visitor, laying his hat and gloves on the glass-topped desk, "I did you a great favor, just a little more than five years ago. Your conviction of me was the first case that brought you prominently into the public eye. I am not overstating the facts when I say you are now district attorney because of that case. Do you remember me?"

"Perfectly," answered Brant, which was quite true. Vestine, Aalborg, Enemark — whatever you choose to call him — had not changed appreciably. He had grown a little higher in the forehead, perhaps, where the hair had faded; had taken on a few pounds of flesh, and showed a fresher color, that was all. His clothes still were of the quiet blue with the faint vertical stripe, that he always wore. He looked content and well-to-do. Prosperity seemed to have knocked at his door and found that door open.

"Are you amicably disposed toward me, Mr. Brant?" asked Vestine, for so we shall name him.

"Sit down, please," invited the district attorney with a smile.

Vestine sat down, crossed one leg over the other, and waited.

"Well?" asked Brant.

"I still have a question before you, Mr. Brant. Are you amicable?"

"Perfectly. To be frank with you, Mr. — er — Enemark, I'm

sorry I couldn't send you to the chair. I did my best to, and failed. That's all part of the fortunes of war, and I hold no ill will. So long as you go straight, and break no laws, I bear no animus."

"Neither do I against you. I am planning to go back to Denmark in about a month. 'My native country, thee,' and all that sort of thing. Before I start, I have a favor to ask of you."

"What is it?"

"I want to get married."

Brant smiled and drummed his fingers on the desk.

"That's very laudable," he answered. "Marriage is often an excellent asset to a man's success and honesty."

"Quite so. Have I your permission to marry the young lady of my choice, under honorable conditions?"

"Certainly! Why ask me?"

"There's a very special reason, Mr. Brant."

"Which is —"

"She happens, at present, to be under indictment for forgery in this city, and out on bail. This forgery she committed without my knowledge or consent, in a kind of moment of inadvertence, so to speak. Her bail is two thousand dollars. I'm her bondsman — indirectly. Well?"

"Well?"

"I want the indictment quashed and the bail bond returned. She could jump bail, easily enough, and I could afford to lose two thousand dollars without serious inconvenience. But that doesn't suit my purpose. First, because two thousand dollars is really money; and second because forgery's an extraditable offense, and I don't intend to have my wife a fugitive from justice. Therefore, I'm asking you to do me this favor."

"Well, you *are* a cool one, I must say!" exclaimed the district attorney.

"Very true. Will you arrange the matter for me?"

"I like your nerve!"

"I'm glad of that, Mr. Brant. It's helped you before now. Please make a note of my fiancée's case. It's docketed as No. 327, for the spring term. And —"

"Why, this is preposterous!" cried Brant, reaching for the push button. "Good day, sir!"

"Wait," smiled Vestine, gently pushing back the other's hand. "Suppose you refuse me, what then?"

"Why — why —"

"Imagine the disastrous effect on you, if the facts of my trial and conviction — the inside facts — should come out."

"What d'you mean?"

"I mean," answered Vestine, with not a trace of emotion, "that if you refuse me what I ask, I shall positively have to tell you the truth about yourself."

"What truth?"

"Truth that you won't want the opposition newspapers to get hold of. Will you quash the indictment?"

"Certainly *not!*"

Vestine sighed, as if with regret for Brant's obstinacy.

"Too bad," said he. "You force me to disclose facts that might so easily have remained hidden. Facts that will forever destroy your peace of mind and your confidence in — well, in certain persons you might prefer to trust. Before I tell you, I ask again whether you will do what —"

"Why, this is insanity! I should say not!"

"It can all be done very quietly. 'No bill' is a formula covering a multitude of errors. And I am prepared to make restitution on the check forged by the young lady. Then away we go, back to Denmark, and all is merry as the traditional marriage bell. What do you say, Mr. Brant?"

"I say this interview is ended! And do you realize you're trying to intimidate me, to suborn justice? Do you know what the consequences of that may be to you?"

"My dear Mr. Brant, pray listen to reason," persisted Vestine. "I assisted you in your marital program, and brought happiness to your wife and you. Now I am asking a little reciprocation, that's all. In the name of your excellent wife, I beg you will allow another woman to become mine, free and clear."

"See here, Enemark, or whoever you are," rapped out the district attorney, "we're not going to discuss this any further. My wife's name isn't going to be dragged into any matter by a man who —"

"Sh!" smiled the Dane imperturbably. "My good young man, I see you are one of those unfortunate beings who can't be led, but must be driven. Well, then, on your own head be it. The fact is —"

"I don't want to hear your 'facts!' I've heard enough, had enough of you. I advise you to go, now, before —"

"The fact is, Mr. Brant, in that famous case of yours I was what your American slang so picturesquely calls 'the fall guy,' that made the corner stone of your success, I was bought and paid for in the market — bought and paid for, like a herring, by your esteemed father-in-law. And the price paid for me was just exactly —"

VI.

"That's a damned lie!" cried Brant passionately, starting up.

"The price paid for me was just exactly fifty thousand dollars which I at once very securely invented in Danish securities," Vestine calmly finished. He, too, stood up. "With accrued interest, and the rates of exchange as they now are, I am comfortably well off 'in my ain countree.' I have exchanged a life of chance and insecurity for one of respectability and competence. I no longer need continue any activities that might bring me into conflict with the law."

"You — you —" choked the district attorney, but could articulate nothing.

"I have purchased a controlling interest in a reform newspaper at Aarhus, Denmark," smiled Vestine. "My wife-to-be, whom you will release, will help me do uplift work — quite like yours, that is perfectly safe and pays fine dividends, as Mr. Cozzens, the Honorable Mr. Cozzens, well knows. As your humble servant and fall guy, I ask you the one favor in question."

"Fall guy, nothing! It's a damned lie!" Brant had grown quite livid with agitation. His hands twitched.

"Please phone the Honorable Cozzens," requested Vestine. "Ask him to come to this office for a few minutes. And tell him to bring Best-policy Bogan with him. Say Mr. Vestine is here, spilling immense numbers of appalling beans. Go on, Mr. Brant, call your father-in-law, who 'framed' you to success."

Brant gasped, paled, reached for the phone, but did not take it up. Suddenly he sat down, with an oath.

"It's — it's all a —"

"Of course," laughed Vestine. "All a fairy story of mine. Hans

Christian Andersen, my esteemed compatriot, isn't in it with me as a raconteur, is he? By no means! For that reason I am so intimately acquainted with the way the first clue was fed you; with all the details leading up to the arrest; with a score of other factors in the case, as I'll prove directly. For that reason I am —"

"Hold on!" choked Brant. "What number did you say that case was?" His eyes looked hunted. "That case you — the case of that woman?"

"My fiancée, you mean?"

"Yes, your fiancée.'"

"Ah, that's better. It is No. 327, on the spring list. I see your memory needs refreshing. I can refresh it to any extent you may need. And you'll attend to the matter at once?" Brant nodded.

"I've had enough of you," said he hoarsely. "Get out! I wish you were both in hell!"

"On the contrary, we're leaving it for good. Well, I'll expect you to take action inside of twenty-four hours. That will square everything. I squared the bank, squared your highly necessitous legal record, squared myself with fifty thousand dollars of your esteemed father-in-law's money — which really bought you your present success as well as my own — and squared your father-in-law."

Vestine smiled at Brant, who, disarmed before him, stood there speechless and staring.

"Just one more thing before I go," said the Dane. "This case represents a very pretty mathematical problem. It is known as the Theorem of Pythagoras. Mr. Cozzens and you and I form a triangle. Perhaps I may state it better by saying we three are the three sides of a right triangle. I insist on being the hypotenuse, or longest side. I'm the hypotenuse, because the square of the hypotenuse equals the squares of the other two sides, added. And I'm going to be squared, now. I'm going square. Hope you and the Honorable Cozzens are, too."

Speaking, he drew from his pocket a slip of paper, a blue check, and looked at it; and as he looked, he nodded.

"No more prison for mine, thank you," said he. "Under your law, a man can't be twice put in jeopardy of his life or liberty for the same crime. Even though guilty, if he's tried and acquitted, that lets him out. So I'm safe now. Therefore, I don't mind telling you —"

"What?"

"See this check?"

"What is it?"

"It's the one that Markwood Hinman cashed. The one that was taken from Henry Kitching, after he had been knocked cold in the alley."

"The forged check that — that disappeared?"

"Yes."

"But how did you —"

"Listen, my dear young man," answered the Dane. "What I got for being the fall guy, and agreeing to be tried by you before a fixed jury — facts that your father-in-law will verify — was a good deal more than fifty thousand dollars. I got —"

"What else? What more?"

"Perpetual immunity. Now you know. But you will never dare tell the world. That would ruin you. But now you understand."

He struck a match, lighted the check, and held it till it flared. He dropped the ashes into the wastebasket, picked up his hat and gloves, and turned toward the door.

"Here, wait a minute!" gulped Brant "What — what's the idea? Where did you get that check — and what do you mean by immunity, if — if you aren't the man that — that killed —"

"Ah, but I *am*, you see," smiled Vestine impassively. "Good-by!"

TEST TUBES

I HAVE SEEN daisies growing on an ash-dump. I have seen per-
fumes made of evil chemicals in test tubes. Steel forms itself under
slag, in crucibles. Freud tells us we are merely psychologically
reacting automata, slaves of external stimuli. But some believe in
free will. Does anybody know anything? All things are possible.

The chiming of the clock in Peter Brodbine's library brought the
banker to his feet.

"Midnight," said he. "Let's be going."

Lillian nodded. "All right. It's time we hit the pike!" She stood
up and walked into the front hall.

Peter still delayed a minute. He remained there, looking round
the library. On a rainy November night like this, it invited the soul to
loaf and be warm. Peter loved his books. When he had been "Tony
the Scratcher," he had always loved to read. He had educated himself
behind barred windows. But never until now had he possessed
enough books. Much he hated to leave them. In a fugitive motorcar,
however, one can't be loaded with books. Everything would have to
be abandoned. That meant pain to the banker. It hurt. In eleven years,
a man accumulated so many things!

His eyes traveled in mute farewell round the room where innumerable evenings had been happily passed, where innumerable
cigars and pipefuls had been smoked with the men of Rockville. Lots
of business deals had been put through there, as well. Now, a smolder
of ashes in the fireplace told where many a record of such had per-
ished. Not that any of those deals had ever been crooked. Not one!
Honesty had, indeed, been Brodbine's trump, his joker. But the
banker had not wanted to leave any records. Tonight's deal was to be
a cash one. Just cash.

The library seemed, somehow, to have grown into Peter's heart.
That heart wasn't sentimental. Never had been. And yet —

"Well," said Peter, and turned off the Wellsbach.

In the hallway, his wife already had her fur coat on, her rubbers,
her doeskin gloves. A well-dressed woman. Always had been stylish

even in the old days. The house listened to the wind and rain. It seemed so empty! Even the fact that Linda, the maid, had been sent away for a two days' visit in Weavertown, somehow made it feel deserted. And in a few minutes it really would be deserted. Peter didn't like the thought.

He fished his rubbers from the base of the hat-rack and drew them on. Rubbers would be necessary, tonight, for more than keeping his feet dry. The banker looked a little curiously at his own face, in the hat-rack mirror. One might have thought he expected the single gaslight in the hall to show him some change in that face. But the light was dim, and revealed nothing. An inconsequential thought crossed the banker's mind:

"Next month I was going to have the new electric light system extended up here to North Rockville, and have lights in the house. But now it won't be necessary." That would save money, of course; and yet Brodbine felt sorry he hadn't had it done.

By the single gaslight, Brodbine could see Lillian, vaguely. The woman was stouter, better-looking, smoother than she had been all those long years ago, when she had been his "moll" in Kansas City. But she still remained essentially the same woman. Determined. Oh, very.

A woman would *have* to be determined, to live as she had lived for the last eleven years, and never blow the game. To work into and mingle with Rockville. You know — Ladies' Aid, Rebeccas, and all that. Lillian had done it. The stakes had been high enough to make it worthwhile. More than high enough. Nevertheless, Rockville had galled her. One can't eternally smoke cigarettes in the attic and blow the smoke up a stovepipe hole. One can't eternally put away the lure of the bright places. The old life stretches out such long, insistent tentacles.

"God, Tony!" she laughed, and her eyes danced. "I'm glad our time's up. If anybody ever did an eleven-year bit, we've done it. Well, it's our turnout, now. Nine hundred thousand isn't such a much, for what we've plugged through. It's only a little more than eighty-one thousand a year. And Lord! what a time we've had!"

"Let's go," said Peter Brodbine, putting on his hat and coat.

He glanced about the hallway, as if mentally writing down for the last time all the pleasant, familiar things, from newel post to umbrella stand. His lips looked a little hard. But then, they always looked hard. They had looked hard when he had pulled that final pennyweight stunt in Albany and had vanished from all the world that had known him — vanished, for eleven years.

Brodbine had gray eyes, cold but businesslike; he had a voice that penetrated, that awakened confidence. His handshake made men like him. In the old days, his greatest assets in shoving his "scratch-work" had been just those qualities. They had boosted him, as well, since he had been on the level. His personality and his absolute, unswerving honesty for eleven years, had made his word his bond. Luck had favored him, too. Nobody had ever risen up in his path, from the other days. So he had gone ahead, following the chosen game of honesty as a means to an end. Honesty had been hard. Life habits cannot be easily changed. But his wife and he had made up their minds to it as the quickest way, in the end, to a big smash. When one plays for stakes that mean a set-up for life, only one policy is permissible. The copy-books all tell you what that policy is.

"Well" said Brodbine, as he turned off the gas in the hall, "you see I had it doped right. Those other times when I could have connected would have dragged down a good bundle, but they'd have crabbed the big wallop." As the old life drew near again, the old speech once more enfolded him like a familiar cloak. "You were trying to wolf it too quick, Lil. We couldn't have afforded to unhook anything till it was ripe. Only a mutt will grab off a hot cent on the avenue, when there's a cold dollar waiting in the alley."

"You can't pull that stuff on me!" the woman retorted. "It was half my frame. I know as well as you do that if you play it square, long enough, you'll sometime get to bat."

"Well, we won't chew on *that* pill, now. The game's a winner, anyhow. And honesty don't drag too hard, either, after a while," he added. He could see his wife, now, only as a kind of vague shadow at the front door. "It's not too bad, after you get your second wind. It gets to be kind of a habit, after a while."

"Like coke," she laughed, "or the needle. Only the pipe-dreams, this way, are the real bundle."

"Yes," said he. "It's a kind of a habit."

"And they get to calling you 'Honest Pete.' After they start that 'Honest Pete' stuff, it's all over but the fade."

Peter Brodbine, banker — alias Tony the Scratcher — nodded, and opened the front door. The November rain gusted raw against his face. It was pitch-black, outside; an ugly night, just the kind they needed. Not a soul would be out, in this straggling suburb. Probably even downtown, they would meet nobody. Brodbine had never done any bank-work, in the old days; but he had dropped phony paper for a good many "box-men," and he knew their technique. Because of such knowledge he had chosen this night of all nights — a rainy, stormy, Saturday night.

"It looks pretty good to *me!*" judged Lillian, who once on a time had been Delia the Dip. She too came out. The banker shivered, and buttoned up his ulster under his chin.

"It gets to be kind of a habit — like dope," he repeated.

He closed the front door. The slight, hollow sound of that closing reverberated in the man's heart. It seemed like the shutting-up of life. Eleven years in a little town like Rockville, where you know everybody, is a long time.

"Come on!" bade Peter, and led the way toward the garage.

They slid back the door, and got into the machine. Their suit-cases already lay in the limousine body. These cases held all they meant to salvage from home. Passengers from a sinking ship take only their best valuables, if anything at all. The Brodbines were taking only theirs — a little clothing, a few toilet-articles, a trinket or two. On a trek like this, planned to carry them half round the world without a stop and to end there in complete disappearance, impedimenta are unwelcome.

Brodbine switched on the lights, stepped on the self-starter and let in the clutch. The car cradled out of the garage and down the graveled way to the street. For a second, the lights touched the rear of the big, comfortable old house, illuminating the summer-kitchen. Above it, the woman caught a glimpse of her bedroom windows — the room now abandoned for unknown adventurings. Brodbine saw, too, and frowned a little, but the woman laughed.

"So long, shack!" she gibed. Brodbine realized her callousness, and shivered. He swung the car south, toward town, toward the bank he was president of. Save for the stab of the headlights, night had everything its own way. The blue light the streetlamps were making against rain and wind seemed only to intensify the blackness. Nobody was stirring. This community was still so old-fashioned that people slept there, o' nights. Oh, yes, the town had a couple of constables, beside Gilkey, the fat Chief of Police who occupied quarters in the basement under the Post Office, where the lockup was. But the Brodbines, who in their day had outplayed some of the keenest "dicks" in the country, didn't give the local Law much heed.

"Looks like a cinch, all right," smiled Lillian. "It's like taking candy from a kid."

"Candy is right," assented the banker. "From — a kid."

They exchanged nothing more, as the car took them into town. There was really nothing much to say. Everything had been planned, rehearsed, lived over, for weeks. And the whole thing was so childishly easy! Certainly Rockville was not to be feared. Rockville was not expecting or dreading any coup. One doesn't suspect one's watchdog of intending to steal the leg of mutton from the icebox.

A watchdog. The watchdog of Rockville. That, in a word, was what "Honest Pete" had become. Eleven years of hard, impeccable work had landed him securely in the watchdog role. Nothing could have been worked up with greater skill, or could promise to be more advantageous.

In the beginning, after the successful getaway from that Albany job, Brodbine had faded out of his old name and haunts; and had emerged, another man, in this remote place. He had found a little employment as telegraph-operator at the depot. After that, he had become stationmaster. Any port in a storm, you know; and beside, he still had a few thousand salted. This work had served only as a convenient blind.

By the time he had got pretty well liked by the business men of the town, for his efficiency *re* freight-shipments and the handling of express, he had conceived the idea of "going straight" for some years and then of gutting the place. All this time he had kept in touch, by letter, with his "moll." She had approved the plan. He had, at her advice, made a play for a petty job in the Rockville National Bank, and had got it. Then he had realized he needed her as a partner; though he had ceased to love her, he had gone to the woman, and had married her. A wife is a prime requisite in working a small town. He had brought Delia the Dip back with him, as Lillian Brodbine. And she had proved a helpmeet, indeed. A smooth woman. Very. She had been enthusiastic about church activities, and all that. Before long, no Ladies' Aid fair, no lawn-supper, had been successful without Mrs. Brodbine. The Brodbines had entertained a little, too, and gradually had become popular.

Brodbine's efficiency, silence, sobriety, and honesty had got him a dead man's shoes, and he had become teller at the bank. In less than two years more he was looking through the cashier's window. The bank had profited. Brodbine had introduced up-to-date methods and machinery; new systems, all kinds of improvements. Bank and town had prospered alike. Then had come that forgery, presented by a Cleveland traveling-man. It had got by all the others at the bank. Even old Dowling, president, had been gulled. Brodbine's professional skill had spotted the fine scratch-work and had saved the institution ninety thousand. That had been a tremendous feather for Brodbine. Dowling had been quietly "let out"; and bank and town alike had rejoiced to make new rosewood furniture for the newly-finished office of President Honest Pete.

"There's McElroy's!" Lil nudged her husband, as the car loped past a wide lawn fenced with ornamental wire. A streetlight vaguely outlined a cast-iron stag. Rockville still clung to wire fences, iron animals and fountains with iron children holding umbrellas. "The Macs'll sit up and take notice, after this smash, eh? Mrs. Mac won't hand out any more of her D. A. R. wallops to the little stranger in our midst — not very quick again, will she?"

"Mac's a good fellow, though," said the banker.

The woman laughed, evilly, in the gloom.

"They won't be living in that big house, much longer," she opined. "There's lots of others that'll take a tumble, too!"

Brodbine only grunted.

"The poor fish!" gibed Lillian. "The mutts!"

Her husband did not answer.

II.

IT WAS EASY ENOUGH for Brodbine to enter the bank. From his car, which he left in the safe seclusion of an alley off Congress Street, he and Lillian had only to walk one square, turn into Hanover Place, and thus come to the side door of the bank building. Here, under the doorway of the Commercial Insurance Company, he left the woman. There was nobody at all on the dark, rain-swept streets; but still his old-time caution dictated his posting her as a sentinel.

His bunch of keys held everything requisite for him to reach the bank vault and the safe. Of late there had been some talk about putting a time-lock on the vault. Brodbine had apparently fallen in with this plan, but had managed to postpone it. That, of course, would have ruined everything. Now, his keys and the combination made matters simple indeed. He had the combination as firmly in his mind as his own name — or names.

"Cinch is no word for it," thought the bank-president. "Anybody could open this 'gopher' with a jackknife, if it came to that." He unlocked the side door, and entered the building, snapping back the catch but closing the door behind him.

As he reached the interior, he paused, listened keenly. His caution, his flair for any possible danger — an instinct dormant for years — had returned, as a tame wolf's hunting-instinct surges back, when the beast is set free in the wilderness. Brodbine waited a moment, peering, hearkening.

Till now, he felt, all had been safe. Nobody, so far as he knew, had seen him stop his car in that alley where he had left it with extinguished lights and softly-singing engine. Nobody had seen him enter the bank. Of that he was positive.

And now? Yes, everything still seemed quite safe. Old Joe Spracklin, the night watchman — what danger lay in him? And there was nothing else to fear. Spracklin, the banker knew, had literary habits; he did a lot of reading in the little upstairs room where he spent most of his time. Only yesterday, Brodbine had given him a set of ten volumes of "The World's Masterpieces of Crime." That would keep Spracklin busy, all right. True, the old man had to come downstairs once an hour, to punch the watchman's register. But fully forty minutes remained, before he was due to come again. And fifteen minutes would more than suffice for the job Brodbine had in hand.

Still, Brodbine — alias Tony the Scratcher — was taking no chances. His return to the underworld life spread his nostrils to the scent of danger. He had not intended to bear firearms, to run any risks of killing, on this job. But now he discovered that he felt empty, lonesome, without a "canister."

"Well, there's one handy," he realized. "I'll cop it, just in case!"

He walked noiselessly into his own private office. His rubber soles made no sound. He slid open his desk drawer and took out the revolver he always kept there. It was just the same kind of gun that certain other bank-employees had, among them Spracklin, Thirty-two caliber guns, of considerable penetrative power.

The "gat" in Brodbine's pocket gave him more assurance. He looked toward the vault, ready for business.

"Damn that light!" he growled.

The single incandescent hanging before the vault constituted, in effect, his chief danger. He had long foreseen this danger, but had never thought out any way to dispense with that light. From the street, a barred window gave full view of the vault door. Any passerby might look in. Still, the chances were against anybody being abroad, such a night. If Brodbine had had to think of only outsiders, he would have extinguished the light and chanced anybody's noticing it was out and kicking up trouble. But he knew the light shone dimly into the corridor, against the wall. Old Spracklin, from his room, could see that vague reflection. In case the watchman should notice it no longer shining, he would come downstairs at once, to investigate.

The incandescent would have to be left burning. Other dangers, however, were few. The two constables were probably safe at home, and Gilkey was doubtless sleeping. Also, Lillian was serving as "lighthouse" outside. One whistle from her, and Brodbine would vanish into his dark office till the danger should be past.

"Cinch!" he mentally echoed Lillian's comment. Already a metamorphosis was upon him, like a chemical reaction, an experiment in transmutation of soul-stuff. His mentality seemed slipping back into the sly darkness of the old days. His instincts were retrograding. Honest Pete Brodbine was fading out, growing unreal; and Tony the Scratcher was once more taking shape. Yes, the test tube was boiling nicely now.

"Cinch!" chuckled the man who was now something of both these men, yet who was fully neither one.

Though it was time to be at work, he felt no haste. He desired to stretch himself in this new warmth of lawlessness. To think it all over; to exult. The kill was certain. He wanted to toy with it, a few minutes.

The whole "plant," from the beginning, had been easy enough for a man with brains and energy. Brodbine had possessed both. He had given them freely to make the Rockville National the sturdiest bank in the county. His bank had become Rockville's leading institution, just as he himself had grown to be its foremost citizen. His going, annexing close to a million would mean the total derailing of a lot of people.

Brodbine knew this. Somehow, he wasn't quite enjoying it, now, as he had expected to when he had savored the exploit on the tongue of anticipation. He was thinking about his wife. About how little — outside of this scheme — they really had in common. About how malicious she had become toward Rockville respectability. Men who rob banks should work hard and fast; but Brodbine still kept thinking. He felt so very much at home, in the bank. It all seemed his, in a way.

Wasn't it his? When he had entered its employ, its capitalization had been only $50,000 and its surplus $65,000. Now it held something like $1,125,000 of Rockville's and of the county's money, private and public. Under his administration it had moved from a wooden building on Porter Street, a rented building, to its own three-story brick block, facing Constitution Square. This was the only three-story building in town, and everybody was proud of it and of Brodbine.

He was proud of it, himself. Proud of the way he had boomed the bank. He had absorbed nearly all the town trade, already, and what he didn't have, was coming. Farmers and traders drove in, these days, from even the far ends of the county, to park their flivvers in Constitution Square, or else to hitch their horses at the iron railings in front of the bank and to do business there. Brodbine had fitted up a room for out-of-towners, where they could trade and gossip. That had brought business to his net. He had got acquainted with everybody. His system had been to know everybody. No funeral or wedding had for a long time been really complete, without Brodbine. Lots of young married couples owed their start in life to him, looked upon him as a kind of godfather. Ever since he had been bank-president, he had always sent a dollar to every newborn child in the county, to start an account with. That scheme had pulled like a porous-plaster. Though not much of a churchgoer — for he knew piety might be dangerous — he had always been "there" when any of the three churches had needed a new organ, repairs to the steeple, or a boost for the Southeast Mozambique Improvement Fund.

As Brodbine had farmed the town into renewed growth, he had likewise made the bank grow. That had made his prospects fatten. All his work had been for himself, in the long run. He had nursed and incubated the county like a hen on eggs. And always, everywhere, he had been just, upright, honest. Not even his political enemies had been able to say otherwise. Some had objected to his having two fingers in every Rockville pie, and to his directorships in so many enterprises; but all had been forced to admit that everything Brodbine touched, flourished.

He had made Rockville flourish. He, too, had flourished. He smiled, as he realized what Rockville would do and say, tomorrow.

Lillian's voice seemed speaking:

"There's lots of 'em won't be living in big houses. Lots of 'em will take a tumble!"

Brodbine brought himself to action, with an effort. How long had he been musing? He could not tell. He only knew he had been hugely enjoying himself. He liked that office, just as he liked his home. The way the desk sat, with the light just so, and the view of the Square, and the swivel-chair with the leather cushion — Comfortable. Safe. Box of cigars always in the drawer, too; and people coming in to confer with him, and people asking loans or advice. Handshakes, and a good deal of publicity in the Rockville *Telegram*. And then, that talk of him for mayor, next year. And friends. Lots of friends. And that house, that library, up there in North Rockville. Disconnected, disjointed impressions —

Wind, rain and, night, like frightened fugitives, skittered and gusted against the windows. The barred windows. Brodbine shivered.

Brodbine sat down in his swivel-chair, in the black shadow of his office, to think. To ponder, again.

"I hope," said he to himself, "I'm not going to make a damn fool of myself, one way or the other. Whatever I do, guess I will be a damn fool. Go through, or quit, I'll always think I was. Which way will be the damndest?"

III.

THE MAN, WHO WAS partly two men and wholly neither one, became aware of a presence in the bank. A draught of raw air struck him. A sound, as of quiet feet, tensed his muscles. His hand slid into his pocket, fingered the gun there.

Then he heard a swish-swish of skirts. A very slight sound that was, but Brodbine understood.

He got up, and in silence went to meet the woman who now was Lillian Brodbine, his wife, and who had been Delia the Dip.

She saw him, vaguely; came toward him. Not even the dim light could mask her anger.

"Got the stuff?" she demanded, whispering.

He shook his head.

"What's the idea? What's the matter with you, anyhow, you mutt?" she breathed. "You've been in here fifteen minutes."

"I've been in here, in this bank, nearly ten years," he answered. "It's a good place to stay in, when you think it over!"

She did not understand, but plucked him by the sleeve.

"Long enough to ha' done it twice over," she added. "Get busy, Tony!"

"Lil," he whispered. "Come, let's go!"

"Well, grab the kale, then, and —"

"I don't mean that, Lil. Let's go — home."

"Home?"

He nodded. The woman stared at him, not understanding.

"It's not so bad, at that, Lil. And this job, here —"

"Tony!"

"And then, wrecking the town, and all —"

Had she dared, she would have screamed out against him, struck him, reviled him. But fear kept her voice to a rasp and a rattle. Snake-like — that was how it seemed.

"Home! You — you —! Gone straight on me, have you? Cold feet, an' double-crossed me an' gone straight?"

"Call it that. It's just a matter of commonsense. You see —"

"You won't, though!" For all her whispering, her tones made Brodbine's heart sick. This was not Lillian's voice, but Delia's. It came to him, from the black past, like cold winds blowing out of a nightmare-tempest. "You ain't goin' to get away with that, Tony! Not by a damn sight!"

"I'm going to stay here in Rockville," he answered evenly. "When it comes to being trailed all over creation, for a little rake-off — or a big one — as against this job, why —"

"You quitter!" Her face looked feline. It only made a dim, white blur in the gloom of the bank, but Brodbine could sense the animality of it. "Quitter! Yellow streak, a foot wide!"

"We've got a good home, and everything's safe. We'd be fools —"

"Eleven years o' this tank-town, an' now —"

He laid a hand over her mouth.

"Cut it out!" he growled, stirring to anger. "I'm running this deal. It's all off!"

Furiously she struck his hand down.

"It ain't all off! This punk town! Think I'm goin' to stick in the mud here? All right for you, maybe! All right for a mutt an' a quitter. But nix on that for mine! I know — I've got you! Got you hamstrung, you —!"

"Can it, or —"

Brodbine was afraid, now. Anger had swamped the woman's caution. Her voice was rising.

"Can nothin'! You ain't goin' to put this over on me!" Her speech had reverted to the underworld. Her veneer had stripped clean off. "I know that safe combination as well's you do, Tony. You're going to make your get, with me! If you don't —"

Brodbine felt a quivering at the pit of his stomach. He had as yet never struck a woman, but he wanted to, now. He wanted to kill. His nostrils widened. His lips grew even harder than they had been in the old days.

"That'll do!" he growled. "Nobody ever threatened me, yet, and got away with it!"

"If you don't go through," she retorted, still in that rising whisper, "I'll blow the game. I'll wise 'em, who you are. That'll be stir for both of us. I'll be done, but so'll you. You're through with Rockville, anyhow. Which way? It's up to you!"

The banker shivered. He felt sick. Delia, his moll — the wife had vanished — was a terribly dangerous woman. He knew her.

Knew she would keep her word. In this moment of something almost like his regeneration, motivated though it so largely was by realization of the relative values of the crooked path and the straight, the woman stood squarely across his path. Nobody had ever done that, and succeeded.

The touch of the gun in his fingers thrilled him. He half-drew the weapon from his pocket.

"Hey!" exclaimed a voice in the gloom. "Who's there? Whatcha doin'?"

They both faced round, tensed to silence. The vague form of old man Spracklin adumbrated itself in the corridor doorway. Brodbine retreated, back into his office.

"Plug him, you fool!" whispered the woman to her husband. "Get that rod in your desk, an' let him have it!" Bold, defiant, she remained there at the edge of the shadow cast by the vault. Her husband was behind her, at her left side, perhaps twelve feet away.

"Answer, or I'll shoot!" warned the aged watchman. His voice quavered a little, but Brodbine sensed the courage in it. An irrelevant thought nicked the banker's brain, as such thoughts will even at life's crises: "Didn't know the old man had the backbone to fight. I'll raise his pay — pension him!"

Brodbine saw the watchman's gun flick a ray of dim light, as it was leveled. Instinct brought the ex-scratcher's own canister to bear on Spracklin. No man, least of all one with a master's degree in the University of Crime, likes to face a muzzle without trying to retaliate. Then Brodbine turned his gun aside.

"Plug him, you damn fool!" exclaimed the woman, this time aloud.

Spracklin's gun coughed. At the same instant, almost, Brodbine fired. The woman crumpled down, with a curse only half-mouthed.

The watchman's flash-lamp blinded Brodbine. He slid his gun into his pocket, and hoisted both hands.

"Don't shoot, Joe!" he exclaimed. "And for God's sake, put out that light!"

Dazed, the old man shuffled forward. He still held the light on Brodbine.

"Why — God's sakes alive! *Your* —?"

"Shut up, and put out that light!" commanded the banker. "I'm boss, here. Do as I tell you!"

The light died. Old Spracklin stood there and shivered with a very cold fear. He understood nothing; and the dark, silent blotch of something that had been human, near the corner of the vault, sickened him. His teeth chattered a little, for all that they were false.

"Keep quiet! Come here!"

The watchman obeyed. Brodbine walked a few steps to his wife, knelt, listened at her heart. He unbuttoned the fur coat, with hands that did not tremble, that silently rejoiced.

Still, he realized, the old man was watching him. There was a role to act. So he started, a little, caught his breath, and tragically looked up.

"She — she's dead!" he gulped, in the dark. "My wife — my wife — *dead!*"

"No! No, no! Don't say that!" The gun shook in the old employee's hand.

"We can't have news of this get about, Spracklin!"

"No, no, no! But, Mr. Brodbine, what was you doin' in the bank, this time o' night?"

"Came down to get some ledgers, for over Sunday. My wife — poor soul — wanted to come along, too. Always that way, Spracklin!" The banker's voice wept. "Always trying to help me, and now —"

"They was *two* shots fired, Mr. Brodbine," asserted Spracklin, now recovering a little from his daze. "You fired, too!"

"Well?" sparred Brodbine, for time. He sensed the different tone in the old man's query. He stood up, confronted Spracklin.

"What was you doin' with a gun, at night, in the bank?"

"When I saw you with yours, I grabbed mine. No man's going to stand still and see his wife or himself shot at, without doing *something*!"

"You could of spoke, sir. Told who you was."

"For God's sake, Spracklin! You going to stand there and argue with me all night? With my wife lying dead, here? Dead, shot down by you!"

"I was in my rights, sir!" stoutly asserted the old man. By the dim incandescent in front of the vault, Brodbine saw his jaw tauten, his combative powers return. "Anybody comin' in here, o' nights, is takin' a big chanst! They're right away under s'picion, an' if they don't 'count for themselves, I c'n shoot, an' not be held li'ble for nothin'. Now, comin' down to cases, what was you here fer?"

"I told you! Help me get my wife out of here!"

"Was you an' her plannin' to monkey with the cash? Hey?"

"Only a fool would say such a thing to Peter Brodbine!" The banker confronted old Spracklin, with tense fists.

"Children an' fools speak the truth. It looks mighty funny to me! If I was to say —"

"Is the vault open, you idiot?"

"No, it ain't."

"It'd go hard with you, Spracklin, if this ever came to court! Remember that!" warned the banker. He gripped the old man by his left wrist. "I — we — had a right here, too. You remember that! My wife was killed here. D'you want it known? Aired in court? D'you know what you'd get?"

"I was in my rights!" doggedly repeated the old man. "It looks fishy to me, 'bout your bein' here. An' they was two shots fired! They couldn't prove I done it!"

The banker shook him, savagely.

"Listen, you old fool!" he growled. "I'm trying to save your skin, and you haven't got sense enough to know it. We've got to get her out o' here, and home. We've got to do something, quick, to clear you, and —"

"Clear *you*, you mean! That's more likely!"

"I won't argue with you, Spracklin. You're an old man, half-broken and not wholly responsible. If this came to court, your word wouldn't be ace-high, against mine. But it needn't ever come to court. It mustn't! It would raise a horrible row in this town, and kick over everybody's applecart. Everything can be kept quiet. Do as I tell you, that's all!"

The banker's voice was crisp, tense. It had become the voice of Tony the Scratcher. Just so had he bossed his "swell mob," years and years ago. Old Spracklin yielded to the dominant influence.

"I — I don't understand," he weakened.

"You don't have to understand! All you have to do, now, is mind me. I'm boss here, anyhow. You're my employee. Listen! Clean that gun of yours. Reload it. Keep your fool mouth shut. *Shut!* Hear me? That's all!"

"All, sir?"

"No. Here!" He thrust his gun into Spracklin's pocket. "Here's mine, too. I've got no time to attend to it. Clean mine, too, and reload it, and put it back in my desk. Do it right away! Don't delay a minute. Understand me? Obey, and it may save you a trip to the chair!"

The old man's brief flare-up of suspicion and defiance seemed to have been stamped down. Spracklin cringed.

"I'll do what you say. But you stand back o' me, won't you? If anythin' happens to me —"

"Nothing will happen to you, idiot! That is, if you keep that damned old trap of yours quiet! Now then, help me get my wife out of here. Out, to our car!"

They lifted her, clumsily enough and with a good deal of diffi- culty, for Lillian Brodbine was even fatter than Delia the Dip had been. Also, she was slippery in her fur coat. The bank door, too, made trouble. And wind, rain, and darkness are not conducive to the easy transportation of the dead.

In spite of all, they got her to the limousine, and into it. Nobody seemed to have seen them. The engine was still singing peacefully to itself, with all eight cylinders. The downpour drenched old Spracklin's head, pattering rather absurdly on his bald cranium, for he had no hat. Brodbine clambered into the front seat. He felt Spracklin's hand on his arm.

"I — I fired at the top o' the safe, sir," said the old man. "I didn't shoot to kill. Wouldn't, the first shot. That bullet must be somewheres in the bank. I'll find it, an' make 'way with it."

"What d'you mean?" demanded the banker. "Mean that I —?"

"Now, now, sir. I'm goin' to keep my trap shut, like you told me to! But, say — one man to another — it was her as wanted to clean out the bank, wasn't it now?"

"It's the chair for you, if anybody even knows she was here! Get back to the bank, now, and clean those guns!"

IV.

Brodbine drove the dead woman home. He felt secure, exultant. "The old man's safe enough," thought he. "He's sharper than I thought, but he won't dare snitch. He's sewed up, tight. He couldn't prove anything, anyhow, I guess a half-cracked old mutt like him wouldn't have much weight against Honest Pete, if it came to a showdown. But it won't come to a showdown!"

Then he thought of Dr. Abercrombie, the coroner. Also of fat old Gilkey, the Chief of Police, who must be notified. Hmmm. . . . Yes, those were certainly obstacles. But what were obstacles made for, except to be overcome?

"I guess I can get away with 'em," thought Tony the Scratcher. "A little bull goes a long way, in these tank-towns."

"There ought to be no real difficulty," decided Brodbine the Banker. "The word of a man in my position carries weight."

The man who was two men drove back home and into the garage. He was glad of the slashing rain that would very soon blur his tire-tracks where they turned from the street into the driveway. Blur them so that, by morning, nobody would be able to see he had taken the car out, that night. On the gravel driveway, the tracks wouldn't show, anyway. So far, so good.

As he got within his own purlieus, Tony the Scratcher retreated into the background and Brodbine the Banker assumed dominance. It was mostly Brodbine who carried the dead woman into the house, via the back door. Yet it was the sinuous strength of Tony's underworld days that hunched the limp body over his shoulder and got it upstairs.

Brodbine laid his dead wife down on the floor, and pulled all the shades in her room and his own. Then he went after the suitcases. He hung his coat and hat on the hall-rack, carried the cases upstairs and unpacked them, working by gas-jets turned low. As he replaced everything, and put the cases back in their respective closets, he hardly glanced at the body. In the long ago, he had seen too many such, for one more to stir his pulses. Beside, what joy was his that Lil was dead!

"Now for the big smash!" said he, at length, and began operations with the murdered woman.

He got her fur coat off, and her hat, and put them where they belonged. The limp neck of the woman, her lax hands, wax-colored face and dully accusing eyes made slight impression on him. He knew now that he hated her; had hated her for a good while. Knew that he had feared her, too, and that this was one of life's most free and happy hours. He drew down her eyelids, however. That dull vacancy of seeming reproach was unpleasant.

He undressed the body, and examined the wound. This was on the left side, about two inches below the axilla. The woman must have had her arm drawn back, when the shot had been fired.

"Not very much blood," he noted. "I wish there had been more."

He gathered up all the clothes, and sorted them. Everything stained with blood he laid in a little heap. The rest of the things he put away, carefully. All at once an idea occurred to him. He went downstairs and examined the woman's fur coat. Yes, the bullet hole showed. He thrust a finger through it, and pondered. Then he carried the coat into the kitchen, and threw it down the cellar stairs.

He returned to the body, got a nightdress — a used one — from his wife's closet, punched a hole in it with a pair of scissors at the spot corresponding to the wound on the body, and put the nightdress on the dead woman. He wet a towel, sopped her face and hair, washed the wound and dabbled the nightdress with blood. Then he laid the woman in her bed, which he opened and tossed about a little, to make it seem as if she had slept there that night.

"Not quite enough blood," he regretted, "but it'll do. Now we'll work in a bit of brandy. Mustn't forget *that*!"

He dropped the wet and ensanguined towel on the floor, then fetched a bottle of brandy from his little stock in a trunk that only the woman and he had known contained any. He spilled brandy on her lips and neck, and left the uncorked bottle on the bedside table.

"Next," said Brodbine. "We've got to have an alibi!"

This was simple. He locked one of the bedroom windows, that looked out over the roof of the summer kitchen. Taking off his rubbers and shoes, he tossed them into his clothes closet, and — lighting a candle — went up into the attic. Here he found and put on an old pair of hunting-boots, with calked soles. Downstairs again, he blew out the candle and set it back on the shelf where he had got it. He went into the kitchen. From the drawer of the kitchen table he took a broad-bladed chisel.

He left the house by the back door, climbed upon the summer kitchen, and with the chisel — working in dark and rain — "jimmied" the window in good, professional style. He now jumped down into a muddy flowerbed, and made deep tracks across a bit of soft lawn. These tracks led to the graveled driveway. Here he slipped off the hunting-boots, and in stocking-feet returned into the house, via the flagged back walk.

He went down cellar, and opened the door of the furnace where a bright coal fire was glowing redly. He had left all the drafts open to permit of the fire burning out quickly after he and his wife had left, so his wife's fur coat and the hunting boots which he had rapidly cut into strips, once tossed inside, were quickly consumed.

"There!" he exclaimed. "They'll have to go *some* to hook me up to it, now. Oh, damn it — those other clothes!"

Yes, he had forgotten the blood-stained clothes. Another trip to his wife's room and back to the furnace disposed of all these. He shut the furnace door with the satisfaction of an artist who has done a good, trustworthy piece of work.

"Now," said the banker, in a very happy frame of mind, "now for Abercrombie and Gilkey!"

He undressed, in his own room, after having carefully washed his hands. He put on pajamas, bathrobe, and slippers, and tossed his own bed quite artfully, taking especial care to dent the pillow. Then, lighter-hearted than he had been in months, he went to the phone and called the doctor.

A sleepy operator bothered him a little, so that by the time he had got Abercrombie out of the Land of Nod his voice really showed a good deal of nervousness.

"You, doctor?" he exclaimed. "This is Brodbine. My wife — she's been shot! Burglar — and she's dead! Yes, dead! Eh? In her bedroom. Just now. What? Yes, I'm alone, here. Mustn't move her? My God, doctor, this is no time for your cold-blooded instructions. My wife — she's dead, here! And you — all right, I get you! But hurry, hurry! What? Ten minutes? For God's sake, doctor —!"

Next he called the stuffy little police station, under the post office. Gilkey, of course, was sound asleep. The old man, however, woke up quick enough when he realized that murder — what he would have called "a genu-ine, first-class murder" — had been done in Rockville. Such occasions to shine were rare, for the local police. And Mrs. Brodbine, of all people!

"I'll be right up!" Gilkey promised. Brodbine could catch the quiver of anticipatory self-importance already puffing the good soul. "Yes, sir, I'll send my men out — pick up any suspects. Lord, sir, I'm sorry to hear this. But I'll do everything I can — the murderer, we'll *git* him, all right. Be there jest as quick's I can, sir. My God!"

"Pretty smooth!" judged the banker, as he hung up. "Abercrombie will be here in ten or fifteen minutes. Gilkey can't make it in less than twenty or maybe twenty-five. He's 'way downtown, and the doc's only four blocks from here. That's all as it should be. Abercrombie is coroner. If I get his O. K. on the evidence, it's all over but the funeral. And I'll get it, all right. A country crocus like this one — nothing to it!"

A few minutes now remained before Abercrombie should arrive. Minutes that the banker used for a complete review of the case. He weighed and tested everything, found no flaw. The more carefully he analyzed the evidence, the more iron-bound everything appeared. Only one weak link existed in the chain. That was old Spracklin. And Spracklin, being constrained by a very great fear, would certainly hold his tongue.

"Nothing to it!" judged the banker, again, and felt at peace.

Trrrrrrrrr!

The electric bell in the front hallway startled him a little, in spite of all his assurance. He felt his nerves crisp, as he ran downstairs, flopping along in his slippers. He grew a little sick, and his heart began to cut capers. But this was all right, too. Quite as it should be. He was grateful for this agitation. What could be more natural? "Buck up!" he growled to his soul. "Buck up, and go through!"

He hurried to the front door, and threw it open. The storm wind slapped the bathrobe about his legs.

"Doctor! For God's sake —!"

"Where is she?" demanded Abercrombie. He came in, shaking the rain off, like a Newfoundland. Brodbine shut out the blackness and the cold. A glimpse of himself, in the hat-rack mirror, showed him his mask of anguish was well-painted. "Where is she? Up there?"

Brodbine nodded.

"She — she's dead!" he gulped, and caught the doctor's arm. "Come up, quick!"

Abercrombie shed hat and coat. With his little black bag — how useless now! — he tramped grimly upstairs.

"Police notified?" he demanded, in the upper hall.

"Yes. You're the coroner, of course."

"Yes, but the police have got to come, too. What Rockville calls the police." His tone held contempt.

"Gilkey'll be here, right away."

"Good! You haven't moved her, I hope."

"No, I haven't."

"That's good! That simplifies matters!" He pulled down the nightdress, studied the wound. "Washed it, eh? No use, Mr. Brodbine. No more than washing her face was, or trying to get brandy into her." His tone was brutally professional. "Bullet must have penetrated the heart, laterally." He replaced the nightdress. For a moment he studied the hole in it, thrusting a finger through. "Just what happened, eh?"

"A burglar shot her."

"How long ago?"

"A little while. Maybe twenty minutes."

"How do you know it was a burglar?"

"Well, you see — the window's jimmied. It's open. Her fur coat, on that chair — I mean it *was* on that chair — it's gone."

Abercrombie walked over to the window, adjusted his spectacles and studied the window. He felt of the marks left by the chisel, and grunted. Then he came back to the bed.

"You called me right away?"

"No."

"Why not?"

"Good God, doctor! I didn't know she was dead! Couldn't believe it I got brandy — water —! Only when I realized — then I 'phoned you."

"Yes, yes. Quite so. Very natural. Where were you, when it happened?"

"In bed."

"Asleep?"

"Yes. I was wakened by a noise. A shot. I sat up in bed, listened, called out. Got no answer. Jumped out of bed, and ran in her."

"I see. What then?"

"Then I saw her — lying there."

"Just where?"

"Why, in bed. There."

"Fallen back, just so?"

"Yes."

"And she was shot, you say, about twenty minutes ago?"

"Half an hour, maybe."

"Shot in bed, there, and died there?"

"Yes."

"By a man at that window?"

"Yes."

"Hmmm! Very odd, Mr. Brodbine!"

"What's odd?"

"Well, the fact that there's a little blood on the floor in the middle of the bedroom, for one thing. And then, the fact that the hole in her nightdress was pierced by some instrument, and not caused by a bullet. And thirdly, that the condition of the wound and of the coagulated blood shows she's been dead certainly three-quarters of an hour or more. And lastly —"

"You're mistaken, doctor!" put in Brodbine, horribly sick at heart "I was here. I know!"

"Yes, and I know, too!" the old doctor retorted. "Look a' here, Brodbine! That window, where you claim the burglar stood, is at the *right* of the bed and somewhat above the head of it. The wound, you will observe, is on the *left* side of your wife's chest."

"But —!"

"Shhh! Don't you think, just as a matter of common sense and wisdom — don't you think you'd better give me the whole story? Don't you think you'd better tell me just what happened?"

V.

THE SILENCE that hung between the two men weighted itself with so ponderable a tension that it fairly sagged. From the library, below-stairs, a single chime of the clock announced the half-hour after one o' the morning. The ticking of that clock seemed measuring out heartbeats of destiny.

"Old Gilkey," said the doctor, with the gaslight making his wrinkles deeper, "will be here any time, now. You've got just one chance — the truth."

"The truth? But I've told you the —"

"'Milk for babes and sucklings; strong meat for men!' Come clean!"

"Eh? What?" The cant phrase sounded strange echoes in the mind of Brodbine the banker; echoes that reached into the soul of Tony the Scratcher. Brodbine's eyes were strange, as he peered at the doctor.

"I'm coroner," said Abercrombie.

"Yes?" Brodbine struggled to read the riddle. Was this threat, or was it offer?

"My verdict will close all investigation."

"Well?" The banker's heart was leaping.

"Just why and how did this woman die? Just what is the exact truth?"

Brodbine's hand gripped the doctor's arm till the flesh gave.

"The — the truth?" he gulped. He felt dizzy. His pallor spread to the lips.

"Yes. I've got to have it."

"I tell you I've given you the truth!"

Abercrombie laughed.

"What's the use of stalling, any longer?" he demanded. "Why did you kill that woman?"

Brodbine swallowed hard. His hands quivered out, to the doctor.

"I — I — damn it all! It's the truth I'm giving you! A burglar —"

"Kick in, now! Kick in!"

Brodbine stared. Not all his anguish of terror and defeat could stifle his astonishment. A voice seemed echoing to him from the shadows of the black past — a voice that spoke the language of the Underworld.

"Who are *you*?" he demanded.

"I? Oh, just Dr. Abercrombie. Why?"

"Say!" And Brodbine's eyes grew narrow, keen. "You can't pull that on me! I know the lingo. What's your moniker?"

"I'll swap for yours!"

They eyed each other a tense moment, like wrestlers watching for an advantage, before the grapple.

"I've got to know who you are, first," demanded Brodbine. "I'm wise. You've hit the trail, sometime or other. Snap out of the bull, doc, and come through! Who are you?"

"Ah, that," smiled the doctor, "would be an interesting question for you — and Rockville — to determine. Some men are just one man. Some are two, or even three. I, perhaps, have been even more. Just now, I'm Dr. Edwin F. Abercrombie, a highly-respected citizen of this town."

"That won't get across, with me!" exclaimed the banker. "I'm no downy bird. Let's have it!"

"I perceive quite clearly," answered the physician, "that the title of downy bird would be a misnomer, in your case. But that doesn't invalidate my claim to being Dr. Abercrombie. This much, however, I'll say — perhaps I haven't always been a doctor. I may have had previous incarnations. Your trail and mine may have crossed, in previous spheres. I may very probably have known or heard of —"

"Of me?" Brodbine demanded.

"All things are possible."

"And you — you under cover —"

"Why involve me?" asked the doctor. "I'm not under investigation, in this matter!"

"You, under cover the same as I am — you're going to blow me, after all these years?"

"I didn't say I was under cover," Abercrombie smiled. "I don't admit I am. And I'm quite positive you don't know me. I'm much older, for one thing. Any —"

"Yes, but —"

"Wait! Any previous incarnation I may have had, may have been when you were only a young fellow. And as for blowing you, to quote your own words, I haven't made any such threat, either. But I will say this, that I knew a bit about you, prior to 1909. And I haven't snitched a word of it. So I must be pretty close-mouthed, eh? Perhaps I had my reasons — good ones — for silence. So now, to get back to the main line of investigation and to resume my previous inquiry, why did you kill your wife?"

For a moment, Brodbine could find no answer. Storm beat at the windows; man peered at man, with soul striving to read soul; and on the bed, the murdered woman seemed to listen.

"You'd better be quick," warned the doctor. "Old Gilkey will be here, any minute now, and I've got to report what seems best for all concerned. Are you ready to come through?"

"Yes. I killed her because I had to."

"To save yourself?"

"Yes, and Rockville. And the county. Everybody!"

"I see. She was forcing your hand, eh?"

The banker nodded. Abercrombie laughed.

"I thought rather she would, in the end," said he. "It was a very pretty problem in psychology. I knew, or figured, you were making a play for big stakes. I was interested to see how it all would come out." He tugged his wet beard, and pondered. "A pretty problem in souls. Very, very pretty."

"You — you don't mean you knew —?"

"Well," answered the doctor, dryly, "you'll notice I never opened an account at your bank. Or rather, after you went to work there, I transferred my account to the Farmers' Trust Co."

"What are you? A dick?"

"No. Only an observer of the reactions of human chemistry. A laboratory worker in soul-stuff. Having been in the test tube, myself, I now enjoy seeing other souls under the influence of various re-agents. This is very pretty, indeed! I interpret this experiment as one in which the male element reversed its usual role, by becoming conservative, while the female became radical. Correct, eh?"

Brodbine nodded.

"A man hates to accuse his wife," said he, "especially when she's dead and can't defend herself — and when he's killed her. But I had to do it. She was bound to go through. I got cold feet on cleaning out the bank, that's all, and she wanted to go through. She put it up to me that if I quit she'd blow the game, anyhow. That was at the bank, tonight, and —"

"And you figured there was only one way?"

"Yes."

"You figured right, too. As the subject of previous laboratory tests, myself, I certify that your solution of the problem was 100% correct. Ethically wrong, but practically right. What was your motive for quitting?"

"Pure folly, for a man in my line!"

"Folly? When you've saved this whole town and county from ruin?"

"The folly of a man who has no real right to a home, and friends, and a legitimate business, trying to keep all those things! The folly of an Ishmael trying to appoint himself a watchman over society — trying to protect what is logically his prey! Motive? There's no one motive — they're mixed —"

"Like all chemical reactions," dryly remarked Abercrombie. "I used to be an expert chemist, in a quiet way, and I know. I'm glad you've been so frank, Mr. Brodbine. If you hadn't made it all quite clear, my experiment would have been spoiled and I always throw spoiled chemicals down the sink. As it is, you'll have punishment enough without my taking any hand in it. The punishment of this community condoling with you over your wife's unfortunate taking-off in her prime; and of living along in this same house; and of keeping on at the bank. If you're wise, you'll take a month or two's vacation after you've dropped your dutiful tears on the grave. You'll go away and ponder on the sublime super-morality of 'the greatest good to the greatest number.' And now —"

Trrrrrrrrrrrrrr!

Again the bell summoned, in the lower hall.

"Gilkey!" cried Brodbine.

"Yes, there's the power of the law," smiled Abercrombie. "Well, I don't imagine either you or I — who've been in life's crucible — feel any great uneasiness about so mild a Bunsen burner as old Gilkey. There's one thing, though, we must attend to right away."

"What's that?" asked Brodbine. His head felt light and strange. His world was spinning, his universe awhirl.

"When's your maid coming back?"

"Day after tomorrow. We sent her away, so we could —"

"Don't expound the obvious. The main factor is that she's gone, and won't be back for forty-eight hours. Plenty of time to rearrange any furniture we change, now, without exciting comment or suspicion. So take hold here, Mr. Brodbine, and help me lift this bed round."

"The bed?"

"Yes. That's the one element necessary, now, to make this experiment a complete success. Remember, your wife was shot here, sitting up in bed. Her wound has *got* to be on the side toward the window. Help me turn the bed, man — turn the bed!"

Together, one at each end of it, they swung it, lifted it noise-lessly around.

"There!" smiled Abercrombie. "Now the *mise en scène* is per-fect. All but that little smear of blood on the floor, I'll clean that up, while you're letting Gilkey in."

He laid a hand on Brodbine's shoulder.

"Just one word more," said he. "We, who have been through the test tubes and have emerged, understand more fully than men who haven't been there, the Socratic method whereby at times an indi-vidual wrong becomes a communal right. We've got to stand to-gether, in a crisis. But when it's over, you and I once more know nothing of each other. The laboratory door, reopened for an hour, must close again — eternally. You understand?"

Brodbine nodded, in silence. Their hands met, and clasped.

The electric bell once more called, insistently.

"Go let him in!" bade Abercrombie, with a smile.

IN MARINERS' HOUSE

THEY'VE WENT and painted Mariners' House an ugly drab and turned it into cheap rents upstairs; also let the ground floor, where the bar used to be, for junk-shops an' stuffy little sea-truck stores.

Once I remember it was a good bright red, with chints curtains at the bar winders an' snug rooms for sailormen — no crimpin' — at the right price. You could feed there, too, front o' the barroom fire, an' get a proper meal for two bits. You couldn't get soused there, though; for they'd chuck you out, neck an' crop, into Commercial Street if you tried to start anythin'.

No loafers ever used to get their boot-toes turned up there, kickin' drunken AB's' sea-chests open and looting 'em, same as I've seen elsewhere. No; it was all straight an' clean an' proper, long as Mrs. Hannaford lived. It's took a mighty long downward slant since them days, Mariners' House has, believe *me*!

Even the great big chimneys up through the slate roof, where the pigeons still strut an' make love on sunny days, has began to shed bricks.

And the old flagpole that once flew the stripes, with weather pennants below, has rotted an' fell down an' been used, I make no doubt, for firewood.

Nothin' to it now — nothin' at all. But in the old days you could see things at Mariners' House, an' hear things, too — things not in the books, things any writer would have gave his eyeteeth to listen to an' put down in the magazines.

I know, fellas, because many's the day and evenin' I used to hang out there. Them times the old hookers an' windjammers fair crowded the harbor an' poked their jib-booms over India Street.

The gurry tramps an' slim liners hadn't elbowed 'em to the ship-breakers yet. An' the bar was 'most always full o' blue-water men.

They'd meet up from Callao to Falkland an' from Cape Town to Nagasaki — meet up, an' touch hands and glasses, an' then go out —

lots of 'em to D Jones, who keeps berths always waitin' at the bottom o' the seven seas.

But there wasn't no disorder — none at all. Mrs. Hannaford was master of 'em all, at that. She was loggin' along toward thirty-eight built, AI, fore an' aft; had a good wad salted in the Casco National, an' owned the place.

"Butch" Hannaford left it to her, that time Swenson caved his dome in with a slice-bar. Oh, I ain't sayin' she wouldn't look at a good, upstandin' man once in a tack or two; and many's the lad imagined vain things the whiles he was roundin' Hatteras or maybe the Horn.

But she was right as a trivet, Sallie was, with clean sailin'-papers, an' not a black mark on anybody's books in this here whole round terra-cotta.

This brings me to what I was a goin' to tell you, now they're all over the bar, all hands concerned — not the house bar, y'understand.

I mean the other bar that What's-His-Name Sir Alfred Longfellow wrote about once in a poem.

II.

WELL, IT'S ABOUT the time "Shifty" Tripp died upstairs there in one of Sallie's best beds, I'm comin' to.

Shifty was mate of the Benicia Boy, you remember — a Bath four-master — the time she lost Trefethen, her cap'n.

They called him Shifty ever since he was knee-high to a pup, mostly because he had peculiar ways to him an' never did look you in the eye, leastways if he could help it.

He was a raw P. I, six or seven foot long, with a fist onta him like a cobblestone an' hair like a livin' flame. But no matter about that.

It's his death I'm steerin' for. The course is well buoyed, too. No danger my forgettin' that!

Shifty, he run down pow'ful fast after Trefethen was took. While I was alive, nobody ever noticed no love lost betwixt 'em, for the old man was some bucko, and him an' Shifty had a few set-tos now an' again.

Fact is, once or twice after a mix, when Shifty spit, they was teeth bounced on the deck o' the Benicia Boy. But all this an' all that didn't seem to matter none.

After Tref hove anchor for the last time Shifty failed right up.

He'd never been no great of a hand to wrastle with prayer till then. But afterward he used to spend his evenin's in port over to the mission loft, an' several times I heerd he asked for special intercession at th' throne; an' at times he'd exhort his own self.

They say he bellered somethin' fierce, an' could be heerd 'way down to Front Street, when the spirit operated right lively.

Second voyage after Trefethen's takin' off I see Shifty had got mighty pickid, an' had a cough onta him. But he signed articles again that spring — 1887 — as mate on the Cyrus Cobb.

Oh, I fergot to say he quit the Benicia Boy right away after the death o' Tref, an' never went anigh her again or set foot on her decks when her an' him happened to be in port together.

There was some talk about it at the time, but folks said it was because he felt so stove up he couldn't endure for to see the old hooker.

So *that* passed all right, an' nobody suspicioned the real reason, which I'm a comin' to now mighty quick.

As I was sayin', the spring of '87 see Shifty in bad shape.

That summer, when he come in from the provinces with the Cyrus Cobb, the hand o' death had him plumb by the collar of his oilers. He'd fell away so he didn't no more'n half fill 'em, nohow, an' he spit blood. But he still signed again.

He was goin' to croak with his sea-boots on, looked like; but he didn't, after all, but upstairs in Mariners' House, in Sallie's front north room, like I told you already.

That November, the 17th, when the Cyrus Cobb come in again on her last run, Shifty hired the room for a month an' paid cash down, an' took to his bed.

He died December 9, about 11.30 p.m., so Sallie was in just a little over a week's rent. She tried fer to have him get a doctor, or somethin', but he wouldn't.

He took them last weeks mighty ca'm, considerin'; just laid there an' drunk rum an' molasses, read his Bible, an' prayed, an' then banged on the floor, an' they fetched him another noggin.

Some of us boys used to call in an' see him every day, an' them as could prayed with him. I was one as couldn't, which makes it all the stranger he sh'd send fer me that last night an' tell me — what he did.

Didn't seem as I was extry close to him no p'ticular way; an' yet, after all, he sent fer me. I'm blowed, fellas, if I know why!

Now, I ain't such a much on this here descriptive business. It'll take some regular smart Alick with a pen or typewriter to set it all out good an' proper.

You ask me about cro'jicks, dead-eyes, an' Plim's'l-marks, an' I bate you four fingers on the choppin'-block I'm there with the goods quicker'n white lightnin'. Or anythin' else belongin' and appertainin' to ships, sail or steam. But this storybook business leaves me on a lee shore with all anchors draggin'.

However, I'll do my best with it. You take it plain, with no trimmin's, an' afterward bodge it up to suit yourselves. That's fair, ain't it?

Here's what happened:

III.

SHIFTY SENT FER ME about a quarter to eleven. I was down in the bar playin' Pede with Lefty Jacobs of the Orient Star an' a couple o' stokers from the old Geranium, the lighthouse tender, you know.

Sallie, she sticks her head in the door an' beckons me, an' I drops as good a hand as a man could wish to see in a month o' Sundays an' goes.

"You're wanted up in No. 18," says she. "Shifty Tripp's askin' fer you. Couldn't you let somebody else set in on the game an' humor him? I'll have whatever drinks you was goin' to order," says she, "sent right up, an' no extra charge, same as I usually get for what's served away from the bar."

She was kind of generous that way at times, Sallie was. I thanked her an' said I'd give my order later, an' went on up.

I found Shifty propped in bed, with his long-necker an' his Bible handy.

Somethin' in the shine of his eye, as the raw light from the lamp hit it, started me kind of. He looked all fevered up, Shifty did. Thinks I to myself, thinks I: "You're close to harbor, old buck!"

So his first words don't take me aback as much's they might otherwise ha' done if I hadn't been expectin' nothin'.

"Come in," he croaks very husky, hardly able to talk at all. "Heave a line an' come alongside, Amos," says he. "I'm dyin' this very night. Turn me a drink, there — my hand shakes so I spill a'most every damn drop! That's right — there! Amos," says he, "I'm goin' to glory before twelve on that there clock; that is, if I git this here sin off'n my chest —"

"What sin, Shifty? Which p'ticular one?"

I draws up a chair an' sets down by the bed, so-fashion.

"My hatches is open a'ready," says he, not payin' no heed, "to let the immortal soul out o' my sin-blackened hold. I want her to come forth a shinin' with glory, Amos! I want to sign my articles with my cap'n aloft," says he, "with no contraband in my dunnage! Lemme clear everythin' out," he says; "an' arter that I'm ready!"

I makes out to grin an' takes a nip myself.

"Ferget it, Shifty!" says I, tryin' fer to cheer him, though in my marrer-bones I know it's gospel he's as good as pork. I'd seen a plenty go, an' I knowed. "Ferget. it! You just got one o' your —"

"Got nothin'!" he wheezes, coughin' violent an' swearin' at the same time. He clutches the Book to his caved-in chest. "I got my walkin'-papers this time, sure, an' you know it, Ame. Reckon I sense the condition o' my own hull an' cargo better'n what you do!" he gasps, resentful.

"I got to have a regular gam with you an' git it over with, Amos. I'm openin' up at all seams; the pumps can't hold me nohow. I'm goin' down, now, inside of half an hour by that damn chronometer!" An' he nods at the tin clock on the shelf. "That's all!"

Comes a little silence, with only the ticking of the clock, the sputter-sputter of the lamp, and the wooo-wooo-ooo of the wind up the stovepipe.

"Down," says he, "same as the Benicia Boy jest missed doin' time Gash Trefethen got his! An' that," he adds, "is what I wants to gam about 'fore I founders. Un'stand?"

"Why, what about it?" I inquires, wonderin'. "What in Tophet is there to tell?"

He signals for another two fingers o' rum an' then thinks a minute.

"Amos."

"What?"

"I got murder on my soul!"

"Th' hell you say! Who?"

"Trefethen!"

"Tref — You're crazy, lad! Why, he —"

"Yes, I know. He died o' the hydrophoby, all right enough: but I — killed him, jes' the same!"

I leans forrard an' grips him by the skin-an'-bone hand.

"You mean that, Shifty?"

"S'help me God! I gotta let it out, Ame! I dassent go aloft an' drop my mud-hooks in the harbor — an' mebbe meet up with Gash himself — so long's —"

He gits a fit o' coughin' onta him an can't go on.

"So long's you ain't told? Is that it?"

He nods.

"More rum!" he croaks "There — that's better. Darn my eyes," says he, "this here liquor's the only caulkin' that seems to hold me a bit. That's right — now I'm good fer a few minutes again. Listen!"

IV.

I LISTENS, with my thoughts doin' thirty knots on a bow-line. Shifty fights fer breath to go on with.

All the time I feel he's crazed — got hal — hal — hallucinations like; is that the word? 'Cause, you see, Tref died natural enough. Everybody knowed all about it. It was open an' above-board, his takin' off was.

Don't remember it? Bit in mid-ocean by his little pet fox-terrier, that's all. They crowded sail to make Portland afore it was too late. Thought mebbe they'd fetch it in time so's he could git the treatment to head it off.

An' would ha' made it, too, only fer the Benicia Boy springin' a leak. All hands pumped, includin' Gash himself. That's the time Shifty busted a ligament in his arm workin' so unearthly hard at the pumps.

They pulled her through, but it was too late! The leak done it. Tref, he died just as they was wallerin' inta port.

They had to lash him hand an' foot in his cabin, an' they say his yells was heerd 'way over on peaks. He busted up all the furniture, too — table an' everythin'.

"Shifty's plumb crazed," thinks I, rememberin' it all. "The bilge has got inta his think-tanks an' fouled 'em."

But now he's at it again.

"Listen!" he gasps. "Listen, an' I'll tell you the livin' truth about that there time!"

His eyes is all glassy now an' beginnin' to roll up, an' he's pantin' like a cod just afore the gills quivers fer the last time, but he hangs to his job.

His fingers is just a bendin' the covers o' the Book, he clutches it so tight I spills another three-spot o' rum inta him an' he revives a mite.

"Listen!"

"Aye, aye, mate?"

"I done it! Me! I murdered him, s'help me Gawd!"

He's speakin' fast now, catchin' his breath between words, like he's scared he won't get through in time.

"It was this way!"

"How?"

"Sallie! Sallie was at the bottom of it, Ame!"

"Th' devil you say! Why —"

"Shut up an' listen! Stow your jaw-tackle, can't you, an' gimme a show? Gash was cap'n. I was mate. Helsingfors to Portland, cargo — lumber —"

"Blast the cargo! What happened?"

"Sixteen days out the dog run mad. All up an' down decks, through the waist, even inta the galley an' aft deckhouse — snappin' snarlin' — froth a flyin' —"

"Cut that part out. I've seen 'em myself. How 'bout Gash?"

"Some of us ducked below; some aloft. Tref, he swung for the terrier with a capstan-bar, by th' mizzen there — an' missed; the cur got him in th' left hand —

"Next wallop he caved it. Swung it by the leg an' hove it outboard. Sucked the wound, Ame, an' burned it out with the galley poker; she wuz white hot. God! I can smell that sizzle yet, fryin' like — An' then we crowded sail —"

The coughin' choked him. I see he's goin' by the head already, settlin' fast, an' puts the raw stuff to him hard.

He gulps it all, an' rests a minute, propped up there in bed, with the lamp a shinin' in his eyes.

"I better git a doctor," says I. "You —"

"You anchor right there, Ame, an' lemme save my soul, you loblolly idjit! Don't you shift moorings now — hold hard —"

"Go on!"

"We'd had words, him an' me had, afore then about Sal — more'n once. Never knowed, did you, Tref wanted to splice her? True, s'help me! An' — an' so did I!"

"You? *Why —*"

"'Vast your jaw! More'n two v'yages I'd been turnin' it in my mind. Fine big gal, money in bank, owned an A1 stand o' buildin's — no man of her own, an' needed one my size. Why not?"

"She ever look at you?"

"Mebbe so, an' mebbe not. But I calculated with a fair show —"

"What you mean? Was Gash on that course, too?"

Shifty nods, an' for the first time I see his eyes grow wet. He looks at me stiddy, too, which is strange fer him.

"Say, Ame!"

"Huh?"

"Any more in that square-face?"

I give him all there was.

"Got more?" says I.

"No. This — this'll see me to port. I'm — 'most — saved now. Come here! Stand by, Ame, so —"

"Let go all hawsers, Shifty! Let her come!"

"Third or fourth day out o' the Skager Rack I has words with Gash in his cabin.

"'Cap'n,' says I, respectful, fer I knowed my place — 'cap'n,' says I, 'would you gam a bit with me, not as cap' to mate, but as man to man? Would you, just a bit?' says I."

"Well, would he?"

"Tref was a square man, I'll 'low, even if he did rough things a bit now an' then. I didn't hold no gredge 'count o' them teeth o' mine he batted out.

"No; the trouble was all along o' Sallie. Well, he squints at me sharp-like a minute an' then he says, says he: 'Fire away!'

"'See here, Gash,' says I, 'how you stand with Sal Hannaford, back there to Mariners' House? I seen a few thing's made me think mebbe —"

"'Mebbe I was wantin' to lay long-side an' take that craft in tow?' he asks, laughin'. 'All right. Fair an' square question. Square answer. You're dead right, Shifty, old man,' says he. 'I do — an' what's more, I will! Next time in Portland!' says he an' laughs agin.

"'You won't!' says I. ''Cause I'm a bigger man than you, an' by that same token she's mine!'

"'She ever say so?' he inquired, earnest.

"'No. How 'bout you?'

"'No more to me, neither; but if a look means anythin' —' says he.

"'I've had a look myself,' says I, 'that's what you're navigatin' on. Mebbe one an' a half. Now see here,' says I, 'I make you an offer. One or t'other of us has got to up-stick an' away from this here course.

"'When we make Portland,' says I,' there's a quiet bit o' beach over on Cushing's where two seafarin' men could meet an' argy out a proposition, fair an' proper like, with their bare fists. Winner takes all,' says I. 'How 'bout it?'

"Split my tops'l if he don't laugh an' gimme the grip on it!

"'Done!' says he, free an' hearty. 'That's the way I like to hear a lad talk! I misjudged you, old man,' says he. 'Always thought you was — well — different — though you was layin' fer to take some underhand advantage an' the like o' that.

"'But now,' says he, 'I know you better. Back on deck with you now,' he orders, 'an' let's have no more words about it this trip. But when we're docked there'll be one whale of a time on that beach over to Cushing's,' says he. 'Come — stir a stump!'

"I gives him a look and goes. An' that's the last him an' me ever — ever speaks the name o' Sallie Hannaford.

"A week later, 38 deg. 26 min. west, 45 deg. 17 min. north, he was — he was hit —"

SHIFTY LAYS BACK on his pillows an' gasps. I thinks it's the end, but it ain't. In a minute he begins again.

"Ame!"

"Well, what? There ain't no murder in that, far's I can see. If two deep-water men ain't got the right to plan up a little shindy, to see who's got a fair an' free course fer a skirt, who has?

"If that's all you got on your chest, Shifty, you can go easy. I ain't no sky-pilot nor nothin', but to the best o' my jedgment, you're cleared O. K, papers an' all A1."

"That *ain't* all!" he chokes, holdin' it off by main strength, while the life flickers an' fades an' comes agin in his eyes, same as you've seed a candle die.

"That ain't all — that's only the beginnin'! So far, all fair an' open. The — the murder —"

"Murder, your grandmother! You didn't bite Tref! *You* ain't gave him no hydrophoby! Come, come, Shifty, lay down an' come round on another tack. Here, I'll git you a fresh noggin!"

He holds me back with a grip onta him like an anchor ten foot in the mud.

"No, no! I had enough, Ame! I'm goin' under now, any time. Water's nigh up to my scuppers, I ain't goin' to drift inta the bay an' go ashore to ray Harbor-master in no stewed condition! You lemme be, now — lemme go middlin' sober! I — I —"

"Yes?"

"Say, Ame, she —"

"What?"

"After it was all over, an' I braced her, know what she done?"

"No. What?"

"Blast my hull, if she don't let out jest one word — '*You*? — an' laugh plumb in my face — an' then bust inta tears! Tears, so help me — an' whip out o' her parlor, where we was settin' an' slam the door!

"She — she was thinkin' o' Gash all the time! I never had no look-in at all, not from the start, no way you look at it! Oh —"

"Come, come, Shifty, this ain't no time to think of marryin' or givin' in marriage. No time to recollect —"

"It *is*! Time to recollect the rest o' that v'yage, when I lost my 'tarnal soul tryin' to git a wench that wouldn't ha' had me, nohow! Time —"

"How you mean, Shifty? Anythin' more to it?" I asks, uneasy, fer I'm a parson if I don't begin to see some kind of a dim glimmer o' somethin' cold an' terrible a-weighin' on that tortured critter's soul, somethin' loomin' up through the mist, same as a berg on the Banks.

"How you mean?"

Shifty, he sort of rares up agin. He grips the Book with one hand. With t'other he vises my flipper till he numbs it.

"I'm goin' now, Ame," says he "Goin', and not yet saved. Hark!" His words come thick, between wheezes. "Hark now, an' don't you stop me, or my damnation be upon you!

"When Gash was bit, an' they crowded the Benicia Boy to make port in time fer doctorin' that'd save him, the devil come to me.

"That same night he come, an' I seen him standin' right there in the fo'c'sle, Ame, an' his eyes was red as a port-light in a fog.

"He tells me what to do, so's I can have Sallie, plain an' easy. He tells me how to git her, an' the wad in bank, Mariners' House an' all — yes, this here same place where he's a waitin' now to grab me, if I don't git through in time!

"Plain an' clear he puts it to me, 'Shifty,' says he, 'Gash is a better man with his dukes than what you be, every time, an' you know it.

"'If he gits to Portland in time, an' they squirt that dope to him an' head off this here hydrophoby an' he gits well, he'll wallop you to a bleedin' pulp, over there on the beach at Cushing's.

"'Sallie, she'll natchally be all sympathy an' interest in him, after his narrer escape,' says the old boy, 'an' that, with the damnation lickin' he'll give you, will land you in the lee scuppers an' him on the quarterdeck.

"'Mark my words,' says he, grinnin'. 'They say I can't tell the truth nohow, but I can, an' do; an' you knows it, this time! You're done for, Shifty,' says he, 'that is, if I don't help you.

"'Which I will,' says he, 'fair an' free, an' no conditions. You do what I say, an' everything's yours, Sallie an' all Pool!' says he. 'Can't you grab a good thing when it's put right in your fin?'

"I argyfies with him a little in the fo'c'sle, there. I was settin' at the table, with the lantern swingin' in its gimbals overhead, an' him no further from me than what you be, Ame, so-fashion.

"We has some talk, an' I makes objections. 'Cause, you see, what Gash told me, that time, about misjudgin' me an' all — an' sayin' I was square — sort of stuck in my gills. But — well — well —"

"You give in?"

Shifty groaned.

"I done that same," he hiccups. "An' that night —"

"That night? Yes?"

"That night, that very same night, just after two bells o' the middle watch, I —"

He coughs somethin' fierce, an' I sees blood onta his lips.

"Shifty! Shifty!" I calls. "Out with it now! You're 'most to port, old man! Let's have it, quick, now — you're 'most saved."

"Cargo o' lumber," he just barely manages to stammer. "I knowed she couldn't sink, nohow —"

"What — what about it?"

"Carpenter's chest — bit an' brace — forehold, out o' sight — six holes —"

He kind o' stiffens out, makes a grab at somethin' I can't see, an' tips over the long-necker. My hair just rises up, as it falls on the floor an' rolls bump-bump-bump — the bottle, I mean.

The wind bangs a blind. A puff o' smoke an' ashes shoots out o' the stove inta the room.

Shifty lets out a bubblin' yell.

"I — I bored — bored —"

Then he falls back, twisted half round.

VI.

Come a rap-rap-rappin' at the door.

I hauls the patchwork quilt over him, an' goes to open. As I looks back I sees one bony hand hanging down side o' the bed. In that grip the Book's a danglin'.

"Hello! What the —"

"Any drinks up here? You cider?" It's Mrs. Hannaford, smilin'.

"Drinks? No, darn you!" I roars. "Say, you send, git a doctor, coroner, or something quick's the Lord'll let you! Shifty, he —"

She lets out a kind of squeal, an' skitters off down the hall.

As I turns back, thinks I to myself, thinks I:

"Lucky fer you, Sal Hannaford, you don't know what *I* know! 'Cause if you did — if you *did* —!"

ROUGH TOSS

THE TELEGRAM ARRIVED just as Tim Spurling, diver, was at breakfast with his wife in the kitchen. A leisurely, skimpy breakfast. When a fellow's out of work, been out of work for more than six months, why hurry? The wire said:

CAN YOU COME IMMEDIATELY CRYSTAL LAKE
RECOVER BODY STOP WIRE DECISION COLLECT
URGENT
    DR SW OLIVIER

Spurling's lip tightened as he shoved the message over to his wife.

"Well, job at last!" he grunted. "And we need it, somethin' fierce!"

"Yes, but going down after a body ain't —"

"Tain't what I like, Blanche, that's a bet. Allus gives me the crawls, handlin' a stiff. But beggars can't be choosers. And then, too, case like this —"

"Well?"

"So much a day. Tain't like a contract job, or salvagin' stuff that the position of it's known. Carcasses drift round on the bottom. Ain't nobody can tell how long it'll take to locate one, and so —"

Blanche Spurling shot him a quick glance. She asked:

"You mean, even if you found a body, you could let on you hadn't and get more pay?"

"Well, why not?"

"Wouldn't that be cheating, or stealing, or getting money under false pretenses? Couldn't they jail you for that, if it was found out?"

"Who's to find out anythin', underwater?" he retorted defiantly. "And besides, the way times is — Then, too, what we just found out about Bill —"

The diver's wife sat brooding a moment. Not even the shaft of July sunlight slanting in through the window could make the table and kitchen other than drear and ugly. With an abstracted air the woman smoothed the hair back and away from her forehead, revealing deeper wrinkles than her thirty-six years should have graven there. Her brown eyes, studying the telegram, appeared to see through and beyond it; perhaps even away to the Arizona desert which alone, so their family doctor told them, could yet save the life of Bill, their only son.

"Yes, it's T.B.," the doctor had bluntly affirmed. "But it's only beginning. Send the boy out West, and you can still save him. But if he stays here —"

"Us, send the kid West?" Spurling had queried. "Where would we get the jack to do that? Us, with our rent three months overdue, and a grocery bill with whiskers on it! Where would we get the dough?"

"Sorry. That part of it is beyond me, Spurling. All I can do is tell you what's wrong with the boy, and recommend the treatment. He's positively got to have a change of climate, or — well —"

And the case had stood right there. T.B. No cash to be had, no job, nothing to borrow on. And Bill, hardly sixteen, and their only child.

"Judas!" Spurling had cried. "What a hell of a rough toss!"

His fist, hard clenched, had seemed knotted against whatever gods there be.

And now, this job! Incredible, yet true. Things, after all, sometimes happened like that. Tim Spurling and his wife, silent a moment in the untidy dreariness of their little kitchen, eyed each other and felt hope reborn. This new job; did it not mean a chance for Bill?

"There, there, Blanche old kid! Don't cry!"

Spurling went round the table and clumsily patted her shoulder.

"What's there to cry for now, baby? Things is beginnin' to come right for us, now, ain't they? We're beginnin' to get the breaks at last, ain't we?"

"Yes," she admitted. "But say, Timmy, how'd you happen to get this here job, anyhow, I wonder?"

The diver scratched his unshaven chin; a square chin and a hard one.

"Search me! Reckon maybe it's 'cause I'm the nearest diver to Crystal Lake they could get hold of."

"Yes, that's prob'ly the reason."

"Here, what you cryin' for, now?"

"I'm not crying, Tim! That's just something that got in my eye."

Blanche dried her eyes on her apron, then reached for Tim's hand a moment, and held it clasped in both her own hands, roughened by dishwater and the washtub. Her caress was awkward. Lack of practice, in the matter of caresses, had made it so.

Silence fell. Through that silence a muffled cough echoed from the next room — an ominous, deadly sound.

"But we'll soon fix all that now, kid," Spurling growled. "Job like this will bring a hell of a lot o' dough."

"How much, Timmy?"

"Hundred a day, at the very least. Maybe more. Depends on how much the stiff's family's got. Even though I got to pay my helper ten or twelve bucks per, there'll be a swell clean-up."

"Who you going to take along for a helper?"

"Jim McTaggart. He's 'bout the only guy I'll trust to handle the pump and hose for me. When you're down on the bottom and your life depends on another guy bein' steady and reliable, the best ain't none too good!"

"That's right, too," Blanche agreed. "Oh, if anything was to happen to you — But tell me, how many days'll you need, to find — it?"

"How do I know? Depends on a lot o' things. Size o' the lake, how deep, and the like o' that. This here job — if I have any kind o' luck — might run into thick kale."

Silence again. Blanche broke in.

"That there telegraph boy, out at the front door. He's waiting."

"Yeah, that's right. Gotta send an answer, ain't I?"

Tim fished out a pencil from his pocket. Bending over the disordered table, he scrawled on the yellow blank:

Leaving at once.

T.H. Spurling.

THREE HOURS LATER Tim Spurling and Jim McTaggart stepped onto the platform of the little station at Crystal Lake. He and Jim helped unload the diving gear from the baggage car, also the air pump. Two huge boxes contained this equipment, at which a duly impressed little knot of people gazed with silent wonder.

"Take you out to the lake, four miles," said a loose-lipped man with a small truck. "Mr. Eccles — him that had his son drownded — told me to git you out there."

"Oh, all right," Spurling agreed. "Gimme a hand and we'll load the stuff."

When he and McTaggart and the truckman had loaded the equipment they got aboard, McTaggart sitting on the boxes in the truck body. Out of the village they jolted and away into the hills.

"Terrible thing to happen, ain't it?" asked Spurling.

"Sure is," the truckman agreed. "Havin' millions, like old man Eccles, don't pervent trouble. Only kid he's got, too."

"Yeah, I heard about it on the train. Only sixteen years old, they was tellin' me. Yest'day p.m. They say he was a good swimmer. Quite a champ. He dove off a raft and never come up. Must of got a cramp or somethin'."

"I reckon so," assented the truckman. "Say, buddy." His voice lowered. "I got a few words fer you before we git out to the lake. Can I talk to you confidential-like?"

"Why, sure. What's on your chest?" Spurling's blue eye showed surprise. "What's the idea?"

"This here is just fer you, see? Not him!" The driver's tone was below the hearing of McTaggart, on those boxes in the rear of the jolting, rattling truck. "How'd you like to clean up a nice little bundle o' jack?"

"Jack? What you mean, jack?"

"A real bundle, that's what I mean."

"Sure I'd like it," Spurling asserted. "That's what I'm here for — big wages."

"Ah, I don't mean wages!" scornfully said the truckman, as they struck into a pine-arched road through forested hills. "How much they goin' to slip you fer this here job?"

"Well, four, five hundred bucks, maybe, dependin' on how long it takes me to bring up the stiff. They ain't easy to locate."

"Hell, that ain't a bundle! That's jest chicken feed. S'posin' you seen a way to grab off ten times that — five G's. How 'bout that?"

"Five G's! Holy cripes, man! What're you talkin' about?"

"Pipe down!" the truckman warned. "If he gets wise," and the truckman nodded backward, "it's all off. This has got to be a man-to-man deal, 'tween me and you. Say, buddy, can I talk cold turkey and be sure you won't blow it?"

"Sure you can — though I ain't agreein' to nothin' till I know what's what."

"And not to blame, neither. Well, anyhow, it's like this. If you go down and make all the motions of tryin' to find the body, but don't find it, don't let it never be found at —"

"You mean," cut in Spurling, his heart beginning to pound, "you mean you'll slide me five grand?"

"Yeah. That is, not me, exactly. But somebody'll hand it to me to hand you. It'll be worth that, to 'em, and a good bit more. Git me?"

"No, damn 'f I do!" the diver asserted, careful to keep McTaggart from overhearing. "Why the hell would it be worth thick money to anybody to keep a kid's carcass from bein' brung up?"

"Well, I ain't exactly sayin', buddy. But if I was to tell a fairy story, kind of, I might say as how once upon a time there was a lady, and she had a weak heart and her health was awful poorly. And she had a whale of a lot o' coin. Well, she made a will, leavin' a big wad to a certain relation. But then her son got drownded and she said she was goin' to change that will and leave the money for a memorial library to remember him by. And the fact that she couldn't git the boy's body was drivin' her crazy, or mebbe killin' her. If she got it —"

"If she got it she'd prob'ly pull through and not die or go nuts. And she'd change the will and the relative would lose the dough?"

"Say, you got a headpiece on you, mister, as is a headpiece!" The truckman nodded warm approval. "You don't hafta be told to come in outta the rain. And if you make a good job of it, why, mebbe that five grand might be stretched a bit, too. Savvy? Well, what say, buddy?"

"Hunh! Gee, I dunno!" And Spurling scratched his unshaven chin. His hand trembled slightly. In his throat, rapid pulses were beating "Five grand or even a bit more, eh?"

"That's right. Think it over, bo, but think fast. We'll be to the lake now, almost right off. Well?"

Spurling's head swam. His senses blurred. Money! Thick

money! It all jumbled up with Blanche, Arizona, Bill and a dry cough, unpaid rent, debts, misery, and despair. And then, out of it all, he heard the voice of Blanche:

"You mean, even if you found a body, you could let on you hadn't and get more pay?"

"Well, why not?" echoed his own answer.

"Wouldn't that be cheating, or stealing, or getting money under false pretenses?"

"Who's to find out anythin', underwater? And besides, the way times is — And then, too, our Bill with the T.B."

Suddenly he straightened up. His brain cleared. The whirling stopped.

"Nix!" he exclaimed.

"Nix what?" asked the driver.

"Nix on that stunt. I couldn't do it. Thanks, a heck of a lot, but nothin' doin'."

"The hell you say! Why not?"

"Well —" And Tim seemed studying his fingernails. "It ain't the way us divers does business, that's all. What we're hired to risk our lives to do, we allus does the best we can. Ourn ain't a gyp game, for any diver as is a diver. So thanks, mister, but forget it!"

"Aw, hell, don't be a simp!"

"Never mind about that simp part of it!" And Tim's jaw grew taut. "I said 'No,' didn't I? Well, that means no! N-i-x, no! So — great weather we're havin', ain't it? Reckon it'll rain, to-morrer?"

MANY CARS STOOD parked near the steamboat landing at Crystal Lake. Reporters and photographers had gathered. On the wharf a knot of curiosity-seekers thrilled with pleasurable anticipation as the truck backed up and as two husky men and a very grumpy-looking driver unloaded two huge boxes. The audience tautened, as the stage began to be set for a stirring real-life drama.

Now, with a businesslike air, a gray and thin little wisp of a man came forward.

"You're Spurling, the diver, of course?"

"Yeah, that's me."

"I'm Doctor Olivier. Coroner, as well as physician to the family of the victim. Glad you're here, Spurling. This is a terrible thing to happen."

"Sure, I know. I heard all about it, on the train and comin' out from the depot. Young feller named Gordon Eccles, just 'bout sixteen years old."

"Yes, that's right. He was diving from that float out there." The doctor pointed a lean finger at a raft with a springboard, some two hundred yards from shore. "I hardly see how it could have happened. He was a first-rate swimmer. Must have had a cramp."

"Sure, he must." And Spurling nodded his tousled head. "Happened yest'day p.m.?"

"Yes, about five o'clock. He never came up, at all. And —"

"Been any draggin' for him?" asked Spurling, while morbid folk crowded around.

"Dragging? Yes. Work has been carried on for hours, but no results. And the boy's parents — especially his mother — nearly insane. Their only child. What does all their money mean to them, now?"

"Not much, I reckon."

"And what," the doctor asked, "is your charge for this kind of work?"

"Me and my helper," replied Spurling, his blue eyes narrowing appraisingly, "two hundred a day."

"Two — Well, I suppose that's quite all right. How long is the work likely to require?"

"That depends. What's the depth, out there?"

"Sixty feet or so. Maybe more."

"Any currents?"

"So I understand. The lake is fed by springs. The outlet is a mile below here." Doctor Olivier pointed. "But you can find the body, surely?"

"With any kind o' luck, and if I have what I need to work with."

"What else do you need besides what you've brought?" the doctor queried, while the spectators absorbed it all with keenest interest. Among them stood the truckman, his face drawn into lines of disappointment and harsh malice.

"What else do I need? Well, I got to have plenty o' rope, and a sixteen-foot ladder weighted at one end, and somethin' to dive off of and hold my equipment — somethin' mighty solid."

"That's all arranged. We've had a float built." The doctor pointed where a massive float lay moored at the end of the wharf. "There's a motorboat lashed to it, too. Take you anywhere you want to go, with your equipment and helper."

"Fine!"

Spurling walked to the wharf end, stood and peered down, inspecting the float. He noted the quality of its huge beams. No cost had been spared.

"Hell!" thought he. "Maybe I'd oughta of asked two hundred and fifty!"

A LONG GRAY CAR swung to a stop at the steamer landing. Out of this car, as a chauffeur opened the door, a man came stumbling. This man was fifty-odd, and he looked seventy. His legs shook. Sunken, dead-seeming eyes blinked in the July sun, out of a lined and waxen face.

"Him?" grunted the diver, with a jerk of the head.

The doctor nodded.

The drowned boy's father advanced uncertainly. Eager cameras clicked. Pencils danced across notebooks. Not every day could Harrison T. Eccles, financial colossus, be caught in agony for the world's delectation.

"Are you the diver?" he asked, in a perfectly flat voice that seemed to be the voice of some queer mechanism.

"Yes, sir."

"How soon can you get to work? It's very important."

"Right off."

"And how long —"

"Well, as I was just tellin' the doctor, it all depends. It's all accordin' to depths and currents, and the like o' that."

"Of course. But you'll do your best — your quickest! I'm not appealing to you for my own sake. It's his mother. She — she's —"

"Sure, I know, mister! Reckon I know what a mother thinks of her son. I'd oughta!"

"You have a son, too?"

"Yeah. Just one. And he's — but never mind. I'll do what I can. Can't promise nothin', o' course. It's that uncertain, divin' is. But whatever I can do I will!"

The millionaire's thin hand went out. The diver's massive one enfolded it.

"Reckon I oughta know what an only son means!" repeated Spurling. "And you can count on me, mister, for all I'm worth!"

Under the watchful eyes of the crowd now constantly growing, and the bitter, hostile gaze of the truckman, Spurling and McTaggart unloaded their equipment from the wharf onto the waiting raft. Doctor Olivier meantime sent for a rope and a ladder, weighted as the diver had specified.

Presently Spurling, McTaggart, and the doctor got aboard the raft. With them they took three reliable workmen to help with the air pump and to do other work. The pump and diving gear, when laboriously lowered by ropes to the raft, fascinated the spectators now lining the string-piece. The atmosphere fairly vibrated with electric tensions of excitement. Never had Crystal Lake known so thrilling a day as this.

Presently the motorboat towed the float out to the raft whence young Eccles had taken his fatal plunge. Spurling had the float anchored there with long ropes lashed to heavy grate bars.

The drowned boy's father drove away. Silent and hollow-eyed, he went back to his stricken wife. It lay not in human nature for him to stay there on that wharf, waiting for those deep and cold waters to give up the dead.

But it lay very much in human nature for townsfolk and gentlemen of the press to snatch all the boats available, and hover around the scene. A couple of newsreel scouts set up a movie camera in a boat and began grinding out footage.

"Now then," Spurling directed McTaggart, "let's get busy and unpack. We got to test the pump. Sixty, seventy foot; that's quite a dive!"

"Think you'll locate the body close by here?" queried the doctor.

"Search me! Might be 'most anywhere, by now. Might even o' drifted out the lake, down the outlet — no tellin'. We got to keep tryin', movin' round till we locate it."

"When is it likely to rise?" cut in a reporter, from a boat that had edged near.

"Can't say," the diver answered. "In this here cold water tain't likely to rise, at all. And, by the way, you get out o' there! Think I want to get all balled up with a bunch o' butters-in? Scram!"

He turned to help McTaggart bolt the heavy iron flywheels and handles to the pump shaft, to test the compression on the air gauges, then to unpack the diving suit.

The workmen were meantime lashing the weighted ladder to the edge of the float. A quarter of it rose in air; the rest hung down into the pale-green waters, so cold, so deadly.

UNPACKED, THE DIVING SUIT sprawled on the float, with oddly turned-in feet, with loose arms tipped by rubber wrists. The suit looked like a fantastic burlesque of a body, a bizarre mockery of humanity.

Then, Spurling laid out the massive metal breastplate and the goggly-eyed helmet, its windows crisscrossed by thick bars. His brain seemed humming, as he worked. Five grand! Five thousand smackers! And Bill with the T.B.! And far below, a dead boy's body — the body of an only son — and somewhere, a mother going mad and dying.

"Hell, I got to buck up!"

Spurling bucked up. He forced himself to unroll and to examine the black rubber hose whereon his very life was to depend. Painstakingly he inspected the lifeline, and connected hose to pump, making sure all joints were tight and absolutely perfect.

His mind seemed blurred and queerly confused, but his hands were deft as he oiled the helmet valves. Sitting down on the float he took off his worn shoes, tucked his trousers into his socks, soaped his hands, then struggled into the heavy suit.

Around Tim's neck McTaggart now laced the apron. Tim Spurling had already lost much of his human semblance, had assumed the guise of some extraordinary monster. He lubricated his soaped hands with water, then drew on the rubber bands that were to keep his arms dry.

"All right, the breastplate!" he directed, while reporting went on apace, and townsfolk thrilled. Even Doctor Olivier forgot to feel professional sympathy for the bereaved millionaire and his wife, in the interest of watching this singular procedure of a diver preparing for his work.

Rare sensation, this; a diver descending into fashionable Crystal Lake, for the body of a magnate's only son!

"Gimme a drag, Mac," ordered Spurling. "I gotta have a drag before I go down!"

Mac lighted a cigarette for him. Puffing deep lungfuls of smoke, Spurling stood up and let his helper fit the breastplate studs into the rubber collar of the dress. McTaggart made the plate fast. Faint tinks of metal sounded, blending with a quiet lap-lap-lap of water round the float. At a little distance, conversation buzzed, speculation passed from boat to boat. Now or then more cars arrived at the wharf. More, ever more curiosity-seekers gathered there.

Bright sun, cheerful sky, and dazzling clouds all made it gay, all of them mocked the mystery of human grief.

"Now, them shoes!" Spurling commanded.

His helper drew on the heavy rubber shoes, buckled them over the clumsy feet of the diving suit.

"Weights, Mac."

"Goin' to use the foot weights, too?"

"Nope. I'll chance it without 'em. Can get round better with just the belt."

McTAGGART FITTED ON the leather belt, sagging with more than eighty pounds of leaden pigs. He fastened the buckles that, in case of accident, Spurling could unsnap in a jiffy for quick ascent. Then he tied the lifeline under his chief's arms and secured it to the breastplate stud. After screwing the air hose firmly to the plate, he led it under Spurling's left arm and fastened it in front.

"Ready for the helmet, now?"

"Yep!" And Spurling, with a final eruption of smoke, threw the cigarette away. "Get ready to start the poison, there. Take it easy, boys, but keep goin'. Start twistin', now!"

As the huge round helmet closed over his head, and with a quarter-turn was screwed home and fastened, he became wholly unreal. His eyes peered dimly from those cross-barred windows, as though from another world.

Two men at the handles of the ponderous wheels, began slowly and steadily turning. Mac tapped his "O.K." on the helmet. Spurling dragged himself to the ladder. Clumsily he wallowed down it.

Now his suit began puffing with air. As the water took him, he moved more easily. Down, down he sagged; then with a crab-like, sidewise motion, slid off the ladder. McTaggart, at the edge of the float, held the lifeline and air hose in careful, experienced hands.

As Spurling sank, the line still partly supported him. Cameras did their best. Pencils leaped. Boats crowded in, despite Mac's snarled warnings to stand clear. With a swirling twist, Spurling wavered down into the lake. His vast eyes of glass and metal blurred away into the cold green deeps. They faded, vanished. A line of bubbles rose and broke, flinging fine spray into the summer air.

Water eddied round the float. Steadily the line and hose, paid out by the watchful Mac, ran away.

Already far below, the diver was sinking down and down, into regions of unreality and dream.

SPURLING FELT not the slightest uneasiness, so far as just the diving itself was concerned. Hundreds of times he had been down, often in swift rivers or in the sea itself, far deeper than this. Many a time he had risked his life exploring perilous wrecks where rotten timbers might have fallen and jammed, where octopuses and sharks might have lurked. This job, now, in a sheltered lake was different.

"Cinch!" thought he. "If it wasn't for bein' a stiff that I'm after, it'd be a cinch!"

How he hated diving and groping for stiffs!

Oh, yes, he'd recovered not a few, in his time, from wrecks. But they made bad salvage. They were liable to do such singular and gruesome things. Under the compelling urge of water, they sometimes moved so convincingly, in ghastly imitation of life.

Once, he remembered, he had been fairly terrified away from a job by a body that had refused to be salvaged; a body that, three separate times, had jerked itself free from his grasp. Spurling had had to come up, take off his suit, and gulp nearly a pint of raw liquor before he'd been able to go down again and discover that the body — an old sea captain — had been caught in a loose bight of rope.

And Spurling had never forgotten that nerve-tingling experience. It had made him corpse shy. But as for the mere diving, itself — why, nothing to it!

"It's only the damn stiff I don't like," thought he, as he slid down, ever down into the darkening waters. "That's all, just the stiff. How I hate to handle 'em! But two hundred smackers a day —"

Looking out through the thick glass, he perceived a vague greenish light, still faintly shot through by slanting sun rays. A certain uneasiness had begun to develop in the hinges of his jaw. He opened his mouth, shut it, to loosen the pressure on his eardrums; and constantly he swallowed.

"Oughta have a wad o' gum to chaw," he reflected. That always helped. Too bad he'd forgotten the gum. But never mind; he'd get by without it. Only the lack of it somehow disconcerted him.

His ears commenced to feel as if he had a cold. But that was nothing. Many a time, diving, he'd suffered real pain, especially on top of his head. When that grew too severe it meant coming up. But as yet, nothing bothered Tim Spurling; nothing but his grim errand.

All sensations of weight were vanishing now; strangely fading away. Gravitation claimed hardly more than thirty pounds, from his hundred and eighty of bone and muscle, from his ponderous gear, lead weights and all. Never did a human being move, atop the earth, as lightly as now Spurling when he set foot on the hard, rock-tossed floor of Crystal Lake.

"Gee! Well, I'm down, anyhow!" he said to himself, as he gave Mac the "on bottom" and the "O.K." signal. Dimly an unreal, isolated, mysterious world surrounded him. Everything had grown eerie and unnatural.

A sense of utter isolation, of supreme unreality possessed the diver. He was only about seventy feet away from other men, but he might have been a million miles. Far from imaginative though he was, still he sensed this extraordinary unreality which always took place in every dive.

Startled fishes flicked away; or, growing bolder, circled, backed, and nosed waveringly about him. One bumped the glass of his helmet. It sounded like a small volcanic explosion. Regularly, tunk-tunk-tunk, something pulsated in his crackling ears. That slight noise of the pump was comforting. Yes, after all there must be another world; a world of reality, where men dwelt. A world in which McTaggart was keenly watching; in which the diver's wife was waiting; in which Bill, their son —

Thoughts of the boy stabbed Spurling. For a time he had forgotten the boy, the doctor, the verdict of T.B. Now all this surged back sickeningly. Spurling remembered why he was here, what he had come for.

"Hell of a job!" he growled, inside his goggle-eyed helmet. "But I gotta do it. We need the money, and I gotta go through!"

He stood on the bottom of the lake, peering about him in that unreal and ghostly dimness. Off at his right he could just make out the grate bars that anchored his diving float, and beyond them two immense cubes of concrete with ring bolts, that held the swimming raft. Vague ropes led upward. Muted though all illumination now was, his vision was growing used to it. He perceived this watery world in hues of green gloom. Sinuous plants waved mysteriously beckoning arms. Off at one side lay a jet-black patch — the shadow of his diving float, far above.

"Where the devil an' all, now, is that stiff?"

Vainly he looked. Nothing at all in guise of a drowned body was visible. He felt his air pressure rising a bit too high. To lower it, he slightly cracked his petcock valve. Crowding upward, bubbles chased one another toward the surface.

The job he had to do, Spurling realized, might be long. Had currents drifted the body, the raft would have to be moved. No telling how much time it might take.

"But it's a hundred and eighty-five bucks a day, clear, for me," he thought. "And we gotta have at least five hundred, to save Bill. Three days'll give us the five, and a little over. I only wisht it would take three days!"

Then, almost before this desire had registered, he saw the object of his search.

Yes, there it lay, hardly twenty feet from one of the big concrete cubes. Dim though the down-filtering light was, none the less that light revealed the son of Eccles, the millionaire, sunk in a hollow amid plant-grown boulders.

The boy lay on his right side, clad in a blue bathing suit. The face was averted; one arm outstretched as if in final, agonized protest against death.

Spurling's first reaction was an exultant: "Found him, by gosh!"

But on the instant a devastating thought surged through his brain:

"One day's work — only a hundred and eighty-five bucks. And — and how about my kid?"

A little dazed, groping more perhaps in mind than in body, he started toward the other man's son. Against smothering resistance at that great depth, he walked with circumspect caution, lest he lose his footing. Once that should happen, quick as a flash he might turn topsy-turvy, hang upside down, helpless and imperiled. His own life — no, he mustn't lose that, now!

Almost weightless, he moved. His heart was pounding thickly as an overtaxed pump.

"Our Bill! What about our Bill, I'd like to know?"

Yes, furiously, Tim Spurling, diver, was thinking about his only son. A sick and quivering sensation gripped and shook him. Only one day's work.

"What the blazes good is one day's work to us, now?"

After all that Blanche and he had hoped and planned on, from this job, just one day's work. What the blazes, indeed?

He thought of Blanche, mother of the boy now doomed to death. Then his mind nickered round to this drowned boy's mother and father.

"They'll suffer, if this kid don't come up. Sure they'll suffer like the flames o' hell, if I don't bring him up. Yeah, but what about us?"

Over him surged the words of the loose-lipped truckman:

"If you make a good job of it, why, mebbe that five grand might be stretched a bit, too."

Five grand, and then some! Five thousand dollars and more, plus his wages for a few days' work — all of six thousand or better! And for what? Why, for just doing nothing at all. For just seeing nothing, down there where nobody could check up on him. For just finding nothing, bringing up nothing.

Had ever a man in all this world been left so starkly alone with his own conscience? In all of life, could any possibility exist, for Tim Spurling, of so much money being won by so little effort? Money, money that now meant life itself to his boy, life to little family!

TIM FELT STRANGELY dizzy and sick. Heart pounding and air pump throbbing hammered his brain with maddening tempo, as he stood there in that green gloom and peered down at the corpse, and tried to think.

Just a dead body, the body of a very rich man's son. That was all — cold flesh and bones. And what on earth good, in bringing that up? Oh, yes, of course, it would give back to a father and a mother the thing they longed for; a lifeless thing, but still passionately desired. Without it, of course they'd agonize.

"But how 'bout us, if our kid dies? How 'bout us, watchin' our Bill die? How many dead boys is one live boy worth?"

Tim Spurling seemed to hear words, echoes of his own speech hardly an hour ago:

"Nix on that stunt. I couldn't do it. Thanks, a heck of a lot, but nothin' doin'!"

And then the truckman:

"The hell you say! Why not?"

"Well, it ain't the way us divers does business, that's all. What we're hired to risk our lives for, we allus does the best we can. It ain't a gyp game, for any diver as is a diver. So thanks, mister, but forget it!"

Already he was stooping to pick up the body. It would weigh almost nothing. A signal on the cord, and with the millionaire's son in his arms, Tim Spurling could in less than no time be back up there at the diving float. Already he was reaching for the body.

But there before him, suddenly he beheld — plain as if reality — the pinched, hollow, and suffering face of his own boy. The terror-stricken and hopeless eyes of his wife. Eyes now all too often red with secret weeping.

"What a fool I am!" growled the diver, his brain clearing. "This here kid don't go up, now nor never! I don't locate him, and no other diver don't, neither. And that is that!"

Still stooping, what he picked up was not the body, but a weed-grown rock. Then another, and still another, and many more. Presently the body had vanished under layers of stones which so perfectly masked it that never could any diver locate it, no matter what his skill might be.

"Six thousand bucks!" thought Tim Spurling, as he straightened up from this macabre task. "I'll put in at least three days, and collect both ways. Make a good job of it, while I'm at it. And any man as wouldn't do the same, to save his own boy's life, he'd be a quitter an' a coward, on top o' bein' a poor damn fool!"

All of a sudden very weak and trembling, he wanted to regain the upper air. Then after a while he could go down again, could continue the fictitious search. But for now, he must quit a spell.

Tim twitched the signal rope, felt an upward pull, saw the lake bottom slide down and away. Down, away, with that pile of stones under which lay a secret that only he knew. Only he, in all this world! Light strengthened, pressure steadily diminished. And then quite suddenly he saw the weighted bottom of the ladder. He grappled it, climbed up, emerged monstrous and dripping, his helmet goggling over the edge of the float.

McTaggart and a couple of others gripped and hoisted him. Up and out he came, while cameras were busy and eager eyes watched from boats and from the float. Sitting down on the edge of the float, he motioned for McTaggart to unscrew his helmet and take it off.

"Whew!" he breathed, deep-lunged and glad of air not pumped through a rubber hose. "Gimme a drag!"

"Find anythin'?" Mac eagerly queried.

"Not yet."

Another voice cut in — a trembling voice, a woman's:

"But you will? You will?"

Astonished, Spurling turned his head. He blinked in the sunshine that cut his eyes after the vague obscurity of the depths. Beside the float he saw a motor launch, all brass and varnish, with a uniformed mechanician at its gleaming engine. In wicker chairs, aft, a man and a woman were sitting — Eccles and his wife.

"Look a here, mister!" Spurling reproved the millionaire. He felt aggrieved, to have these two hanging round while he was at work. "See here, now. You hadn't oughta be here. This here ain't no place for you two!" His clumsy, rubber-gloved hand sketched a crude gesture. "No place, 'tall!"

"I know it," the magnate assented, while listeners stretched their ears. Eccles, for all the heat of that July day, was shivering. His body shook as with a palsy. "I know it, but —"

"I had to come. I had to!" put in his wife. "I couldn't stay away and wait —"

Spurling's lip tightened with acid disapproval. An extraordinary and grotesque figure — with his head, seemingly far too small, projecting up out of that vast suit — he looked at the dead boy's mother. And what he saw was human agony, raw and bleeding.

The diver understood. The woman's sunken eyes and pale lips, her deep-lined face, told the whole story. This story was underscored by her quivering fingers that tightly clutched the arms of the wicker chair.

"If you only knew," the mother half-whispered. "If you could only understand what it means to lose an only son!"

"Reckon I do ma'am," answered the diver. "Or reckon I will, pretty soon."

"Why — how —"

"Well, I got a kid o' my own, see? 'Bout the same age as yours was, and he's dyin'. Arizona's all that'll save him. But Arizona ain't for us. Huh! Fat chance we got o' that!"

"Oh!" breathed Mrs. Eccles comprehendingly, while the reporters pounced on a wonderful human-interest story. "You mean you've got a —"

"Tell me," the millionaire brusquely cut in. "You haven't found anything, yet? No sign, no indication?"

"Nothin', so fur. Not yet."

"But you will? You're going down again, right away?"

"Yeah, pretty soon. Quick as I rest up, a little, and get this cold out o' my bones."

"And you'll find my son?" asked the mother. "You will, won't you?"

"Well, gee, I'll try."

"No, no! Promise you'll find him. Oh, don't you see, you've got to?"

Tim Spurling began to feel very queer and sick again. Something seemed to have hold of his guts and to be twisting them. He blinked as he looked that woman fair in the eyes. Between the float and the motor launch extended a distance of not more than four feet. Between Tim Spurling, workman, and those two millionaires, stretched infinity. But something strove to bridge that infinity.

Under the compulsion of this something, under the fever of that stricken woman's look — that appealing, agonized, crucified look — Spurling felt his plans all riven, cast awry and wrecked.

"Hell!" he tried to rally himself. "Don't be a quitter and a fool!"

But it was no good. For the woman was speaking again.

"Your own boy — you say he's very ill?"

"Yes. T.B."

"What's his name?"

"William. But o' course we call him just Bill."

"And how old?"

"Sixteen, ma'am. Your boy — same age?"

She nodded. He saw tears gleaming in her faded eyes.

"Please get away from here," he begged. "I'm goin' down again right away, and when I come up mebbe you better not be here." He appealed to the millionaire. "See here, Mr. Eccles. Get her out o' here. Won't you take her away, please?"

"He's right, Valerie," the magnate assented. "We really ought to go." He gave a word of command to the mechanic at the engine. Then, to Spurling: "You're going down again, right now?"

"Yeah. Just as quick's I have a smoke and a bit of a rest. And you can count on me. I'll do the best I can!"

As the powerful engine started, and the motorboat purred away with those two lonely, sorrowful, rich, death-stricken figures, Tim Spurling gazed after them with tragic eyes.

"The best I can, for you," he thought. "That means the worst for us!" Aloud: "You there, Mac — light me a tack, can't you? Gee, that water's awful cold, down there. I sure need a smoke. I sure need it worse'n I ever needed one in all my life!"

TIM SPURLING, that same evening, stood on the platform of the Crystal Lake station with McTaggart, his helper. Their diving gear, all boxed up again, was waiting to be lifted aboard the baggage car of the 7:17, that had already whistled far up Swiftwater Valley.

"Damn short job, Tim," Mac was complaining. "Seems like we ain't got no luck at all."

"Mebbe yes, mebbe no. What's good for one, is bad for another. Everybody can't have all they want."

"Sure, I know. But —"

Down the road swept a long gray car. It slowed, stopped at the station. A chauffeur opened its door. Out stepped Eccles.

The last fading of sunset over the mountains showed his face, which though still grief-ravaged was more at peace. He even managed a wan bit of a smile as he came toward the diver.

"I wanted to thank you again, before you left," he said, quite simply. "We'll never forget it, my wife and I. Never forget what you've done for us."

"Oh, that? Well, it's just my job, I reckon."

"Perhaps. But at any rate, we want to send your boy something. You'll take it to him, won't you?"

"Send my boy somethin'?" And Spurling's eyes widened. McTaggart was all curiosity. "Why — what could —"

"It's a memorial. Something in memory of our own lad."

The envelope from Eccles's pocket passed to Tim Spurling's hand. Amazed, the diver stared at it.

"This here; it's —"

"Call it life, if you will," smiled Eccles. "It's a check made out to William Spurling. I've signed it. Your boy can fill in the amount. Be sure he makes it enough to get him well and strong. To keep his hold on life — life that, once gone, can never be brought back by all the millions in this world!"

More loudly echoed the train whistle. A glimmering headlight sparkled into view.

"Why, my gosh, I — I been paid, already," stammered the diver. "I can't take this and —"

"You're not taking it. It's your boy's. Goodbye, Spurling, good luck to you and yours!"

A handclasp. A silent look that passed, not now between workman and millionaire, but from man to man, father to father. Then Eccles, turning, was gone.

The headlight glare strengthened. Brakes began to grind. The train slowed at the station.

"Gee whiz, Tim!" cried McTaggart, as his chief's face was for a moment brilliantly illuminated. "What the devil? Why, you're cryin'!"

"The hell I am!" Spurling indignantly retorted. "It's just a cinder in my eye. This damn soft coal, and all! If you don't know when a feller's got a cinder in his eye — Say, gimme a drag, can't you? I sure need it!"

AFRICA

"SEE THERE? That's Africa!"

Dr. Paul Willard gestured far across the night to where, in the vast dark, a spurt of flame glowed like a blood-ruby, died, then trembled forth again.

"Africa?" the girl questioned vaguely. A nameless awe crept round her heart, in presence of that unseen emptiness looming away to the inverted bowl of sky — a fathomless sky, spattered with great refulgent stars, among which, overhead, the funnels of the Sutherland traced smoky patterns. "Africa?"

"A little corner of it, anyway," the doctor answered, smiling at her tone. "Cape Roxo light. By two bells of the middle watch we'll be off the coast of Guinea, running through Bissagos Islands — a bad place at best. I never liked it, and I've surgeoned on 'old Suth' for more than seven years. Don't like it now, its reefs and cannibal wreckers and all, even with Captain Lockhart on the bridge."

The girl made no answer, but she leaned her arms across the rail, swaying as the ship rolled, and gazed out into the unknown. Steadily the Strathglass liner clove the fugitive seas, creaming them astern in surges that hissed away into the black.

He risked a side glance at her.

Never had she seemed quite so beautiful to him as under the lantern light which gleamed upon her heavy yellow braids of hair, her frost-white gown. At sight of her delicate, somewhat pale face, his smile waned. No living man — least of all Willard, in the passion which had obsessed him ever since Ethel Armstrong and her crippled uncle had set foot upon the Sutherland's deck — could have felt amusement in presence of that gentle, earnest seriousness.

"Somehow, do you know," she mused at length, "I feel a bit afraid? It's all so empty! And just to know that Africa is over there." A gesture rounded out the thought. "I sha'n't quite like it till we're at the quay in Cape Town."

"When you'll immediately forget the trip, the boat, and — everyone on board?" he led along; but she ignored the opening. Her mood was far from banter. The doctor, too, repented of his speech, the clumsiness of which jarred upon the majesty and wonder of that tropic night. "Oh, well, you'll see things differently tomorrow," he retrieved himself. "Quite differently, when the big red sun rolls up over the coast and splashes gold across the sea."

"Perhaps," she half assented. "But tomorrow is so far away. I think I'll go below. This air stifles me."

He nodded.

"Yes; I understand. I used to feel it so myself, before I got quite used to it." His powers of speech had never seemed more pitifully crude.

He helped her down the steep companionway. Then, after a per-functory good night from her, came up again to the quarterdeck.

"Great guns, what gloom!" he muttered. "Why, India ink is pale beside it. I don't half like the way these offshore swells are running, either — with Bissagos still ahead of us. Can't say I'm used to this particular bit of Africa even now. No wonder that she — Ethel — feels so shuddery."

A moment he pondered in silence.

"That's an upper-class privilege, anxiety is. A mere proletarian like me has no right to it. No, nor yet to look at an upper-class woman. For such, we aren't real men — just official objects."

He leaned upon the railing where her arms had lain, and for a long time stared off across the dark where, on Cape Roxo, winked that dim, retreating eye of flame.

II.

THE DOCTOR found no sleep till long past midnight. Even with his cabin window slid far back, the tepid land breeze choked him, and his thoughts were weft of hot rebellion, longings, and misery. He tossed wide-eyed in his berth, heard the ship's bell dole out the eternal hours, then the halves, torturing himself with images of Cape Town and the approaching separation, which (only too well he knew) must be forever. Midnight was long gone, when he lost himself in trou-blous dreams of distant inaccessible things, never to be reached by him.

Toward early morning something flung him back to consciousness — a grinding, raking craunch that shivered the whole fabric of the ship, and roused him to the knowledge he was struggling on his cabin floor, which slanted dizzily. He clambered up, mazed and witstruck for a moment, groped for the electric-button, and snapped on the light.

As the glare dazzled him, the Sutherland pitched nauseously again; and far below he heard a hideous gnawing and rasping, as of stony Titan jaws devouring steel. Then came sharp cries, oaths, and orders hoarsely bawled, and heavy feet that ran unsteadily along the decks. The pulsing engines suddenly grew still.

"Bissagos Reef! Ethel!" These were his only thoughts.

He leaped into some clothes, snatched his revolver, jerked open the cabin door, and ran out in his shirt-sleeves to the main saloon. It was already filled with grotesque, excited passengers. A babel swelled tumultuously, with high-pitched questions, curses, and screams.

"Steady!" he shouted. "Steady, now! No danger if you all keep cool!"

Hands clutched at him; he staved them off. "Lord!" thought he. "What cattle human beings in a panic are!"

He heard the purser's voice that reinforced his own — heard other officers — knew that for a moment his presence might be spared.

"I must go!" he told himself; for in the thickening mob he caught no glimpse of Ethel or the invalid.

"I've got to find them anyway!"

He shoved by main force, along the up-tilted floor, toward their cabins. From behind him, on the aft staircase, Captain Lockhart's mellow Scotch voice boomed out: "We're good for fufteen mennets yet! No danger if ye'll tak' it easy — all han's to th' boats! *Weemen fairrst!*"

Suddenly he came on Ethel and her palsied uncle. The old man's halting steps had held her back. A flash of potent admiration lightened through Willard's soul at the vision of the girl, pale and afraid, yet not startled or hastened from her duty.

She came onward, helping the pitiful, twisted figure, step by step — a figure doubly grotesque now, in scant, disheveled clothing, with sweat of pain on the knit brow and terror staring from the widened eyes. She looked, the doctor thought, most dignified and noble in her long, loose dressing gown, over which the yellow braids hung to below her girdle. A sort of fine simplicity enshrouded her. And though he had witnessed bold, hard men in peril, he thought that never had he seen so brave a thing as that gently bred girl holding back her steps, timing her pace to the hobbling of the senile creature who now clung to her for safety.

"What is it — tell me! Are we going down?" she cried to him, her voice trembling a little, but quite clear above the uproar of the crowd or the grinding and tearing of the ship. Her look was full of confidence; even in her fear he found no trace of panic. "Are we lost? What's happened, can you tell me?"

"We're on Bissagos — probably no danger." His body shielded her from the stampeding pack that weltered past them, herded by a dozen of the officers and crew. His nerves were ice. He felt nothing save joy and high elation at this chance to save her life, at this thought that Ethel now was looking up to him, trusting him for guidance and deliverance.

"We mayn't break up — for some time yet!" he shouted, bending toward her. "No danger — lots of boats — the mainland near! Come on, though — there's no time to lose!"

He stooped and gathered the cripple in his arms, then lurched ahead through the wild mob. Ethel followed; he felt the grasp of her hand upon his shoulder, and strange, mad thoughts seethed up in him.

Thus presently, jostling and buffeted, they won through the panic and the uproar of the open lower deck, which shelved off sickeningly to the very water's edge.

The night still gloomed impenetrable round the wounded ship. The wind had risen and whipped furiously the wild, green flares which flung sick shadows over the features of the dead.

Momentarily the waves boiled in spume-vortices over the sunken reef, sweeping the bulwarks, drenching the mad throng. At every heave and slide of the impaled monster a ghastly discord rose — "She's going! Breaking up!" It mingled with the liner's sirens and exhaust, which were ripping the sky with diapasons of appeal.

A rocket screeched aloft, and by its glare the doctor saw a slashing, clawing frenzy at the rail — saw the davits rock and shudder as the boats were wrenched outboard and the horde swarmed them, bursting all constraint.

"No chance for us there — with your uncle." Willard made her understand. "They'd crush him in a second. We'll have to wait."

He saw her nod. "Talk about women being cowards!" flashed the thought through his mind.

Drawing her back into the shelter of a bulk, he put the cripple gently down. The old man, stunned, said nothing, but crouched low, with blinking eyes. Willard and the girl leaned up against the wall, bracing their feet upon the deck, which every moment settled at a steeper pitch.

Now they could look down on the hideous fight. They saw the captain's huge frame overtopping all, dominant as his voice that blared out in command. They caught a gleam of pistol steel in his hand — a spike of flame — and someone pitched across the rail.

"Bairns and th' weemen fairrst!" his brave old sea cry rang. Then, like lightning, a sudden something smote the captain's head, and he was seen no more. Hell burst its bounds; panic reaped its certain due.

III.

"DON'T LOOK! You mustn't!" Willard cried, shielding from her the tragedy of the long-boat as a tackle jammed and spilled two-score clutching, yelling creatures in the swirl. The boat flailed — a giant pendulum — and shaking loose the few that clung to thwarts or gunwales, splintered to fragments on the liner's iron skin.

An instant, black, fighting things were sown broadcast upon the roaring sea — things that shrieked, went down bubbling, rose, then, with crisped fingers, disappeared forever.

"There's been an accident — don't look!"

"I'm not afraid," he heard her answer, but the hand that grasped his arm trembled. He loved her for the very fear she knew so well to hold in leash.

A shudder ran through the wreck — a roar that boomed above the sirens' bellowing — then, where the bows had been, gaped a vast black emptiness, with death-screams choked by upswirling brine. A third of the whole ship had broken free and, with its fearful toll, had foundered like a plummet.

The Sutherland, eased by this loss, ground back upon the reef more firmly than before, and settled at a safer pitch, but her survivors deemed their end was now upon them, and fought each other starkly at the boats. All but one of the green flares had burned away, and by this ghastly dim virescence Willard saw men trampled and women hurled aside.

"Safer aboard than anywhere with madmen!" he cried in the girl's ear. "Don't move! Stay where you are!"

He drove down into the wolf-pack — his duty called him there — and smote with hard fists that came back reddened from his blows, striving to scatter the crazed brutes. But in the dark and tumult he could compass nothing. A blow clipped his temple; he felt the blood run hot, but he only dashed it from his eyes and struck the harder, striving to wedge through and split the mob.

He saw foul knife-play, heard the first mate grunt and double up, got sights of hands that strangled and glimpsed blind primitive anarchy as a second boat was launched.

It foundered straightway, from gross overcrowding. Amid the drowning wretches, breaking off their hand-grasps, a third boat was got away with only five oars, her gunwales shipping water at each sea. Then went the life-raft. He helped fling it overboard, aided some to jump in safety, and vainly tried to hold back others who leaped out at random — who missed and sank, with never a human hand held out to them for salvage.

"Better stay here! Safer on the ship!" he shouted to the lessening fugitives, but no one heeded him. When at last they all were gone — some to death, some to uncertain struggles with the night and the sea — when all had disappeared save a few limp figures rolling in the scuppers, he climbed back, bleeding, up the slippery deck to Ethel.

He found her in the bulkhead corner, kneeling in the gloom over a prostrate something that neither stirred nor spoke.

"What! Can I help?" he cried.

She shook her head, raising her hand silently, and he forbore. He understood. The old man's heart had lashed itself to bursting with the panic and the stress. Now, out of all the throng, only one woman and one man were left.

The doctor's wisdom kept his lips from platitudes. He turned, and left Ethel to herself a moment, gazing off landward. The ship was utterly dark now, for the last flare had burned to ash, the dynamos had stopped, and all the lights were dead. The steam-pipes' roar had dwindled to a sibilant murmur, drowned by the lash and crumble of the surges on the reef. Under the great passionless stars the wreck lay spent and weary, crushed to death, unmoved by even the heaviest seas.

Quite suddenly the doctor noticed a little speck of light far in the gloom, then another — many specks, that lay where he half guessed the shore must be. Puzzled, he knit his brows.

"It can't be that any have reached land yet. Those can't be fires. Never knew campfires to crawl that way."

Dully he watched the sparks creep, come together, then separate. They almost seemed to be advancing toward the ship.

Then the truth hit him, and he stumbled back.

"Merciful Heaven! the Guinea blacks — the wreckers of Bissagos!"

IV.

HE STOOPED to Ethel tenderly. "Listen," said he. "We must get away from here. It's death to stay!"

She clung to him. He drew her up — away. She was only a blur in the night, but intuition told him that her face was wet with tears.

"Death?" she asked. "The wreck won't last till morning?"

"It's not that. There's something — something else. You'd better know at once. See there — off there to shoreward?"

"Those lights, you mean?"

"Lights, yes. They're torches — in canoes. They're coming. They mustn't find us here, or —"

"I understand. But can we go, and leave the — the —"

"Nobody must be left. There couldn't be a finer burial than the sea! I'll take you into the saloon, then come back here and do what must be done."

She understood, and yielded nobly. He led her off along the steep deck, after a silent moment by her uncle's body. He brought her safely to the main saloon, struck a match and found his bearings.

"All you need do is sit quite still in here. I won't be gone five minutes." Then he left her.

The work was harder than he had expected, for there was a lantern to be found and lighted, and — there were other difficulties. After a while the task was done.

When he came back to her, his pockets crammed with provisions and cartridges, a bandolier of canvas supporting revolvers and two magazine-rifles, she greeted him with a pale, thin smile. By the lantern light that glimmered sickly through the mocking splendor of the place, he saw her eyes brimming with tears, but she was calm and full of courage.

"We've got to find and launch a boat, or something, right away."

"Come, then, let's be about it," she replied. "There can't be many boats left, can there?"

"Hardly two or three. The port-side's stripped. We'll soon find out."

He helped her up across the saloon floor, which slanted like a house roof, and they issued out upon the larboard side. The wind could not strike here; and the waves, too, thirty-odd feet below, broke with less furious lashings.

Willard held the lantern high with his right hand. His left clutched the rail. Ethel steadied herself on him. Thus they worked their way slowly aft, stumbling over twisted cordage, litter, flotsam and jetsam of the tragedy.

As they neared the first boat Willard's heart died within him. What he might have guessed was true — the careening of the ship had swung the boats far inboard against their davits, so that nothing short of half a dozen men could now have got them over the rail, even had not the falls been twisted into knots and tangles.

He knew at once the prime futility of an attempt. Even to have got a life-raft over they must have rigged tackles, and time was now so short. A real fear shuddered through his veins. Too well he knew what manner of men the Guinea wreckers were. His hand slid, as by instinct, to the butt of his revolver. Before a single black should come nigh her he knew a better way.

"Impossible?" asked Ethel almost coolly. "Perhaps there's something better at the stern."

They forced a way, sliding, slipping, and clinging to whatever handholds offered. Under the counter they heard the waves run hissing. The wind whipped them as they worked out from the shelter of the after-cabin; it blew the lantern out. And as they stopped, breathing heavily in the dark, they saw once more the dancing fire sparks, heaving and tossing with the waves, and drawing very nigh. They could even see that the sparks were torches, harried by the wind; and once, in a lull, they heard a wild-pitched, minor chant that wailed and mourned across the vacant reaches of the night, with throbbings of many cadent drums.

The woman trembled at this sound, and Willard drew her close to him.

"Don't be afraid," he soothed her. "They shall never get you."

"Swear to that."

"I needn't. You know how true it is."

"No time, now?"

"No time. We'll have to hold the fort. They probably don't know we're here, so it'll be a fine surprise party. Lots of arms on board. You can shoot?"

"Try me."

Thus, on the instant, their campaign took form.

V.

"THEY'LL BOARD US midships on the port side," Willard planned. "They're after loot, and — and — and — well — edibles. Now we, I take it —"

"Can barricade the stern here?"

"Yes — rake 'em down by dozens. Except for knives and assegais, they're probably not armed."

"How many do you make them?"

"A good thousand. See, there must be more than fifty of those big sea-going *barracas*. But what are a thousand naked blacks against magazine rifles? They can't rush us all at once. Come, though," he added hastily, "this won't do. We've to get things ready for 'em — quick, at that."

He dragged up cordage, with her help; piled sail-cloth, debris, chains, anything that fell to hand in the port and starboard gangways. And thus they built a strong, entrenched position, whence they could sweep unmercifully the narrow approaches. By the vague light of the stars they toiled, and saw their work was good.

"We'll lie low now," panted the doctor. "If they don't see us, well and good. Otherwise a finish fight. In case they drive us, there's the aft companion to the upper deck. We can make a mighty fine killing from up there before they ever get us."

Without another word he drew from his pockets box on box of cartridges, broke the seals, and poured them out upon the deck. He set to loading all his arsenal, then laid part at the starboard barricade, the rest to port. Then, where some sailcloth touched the wooden cabin, he drenched the place with lantern oil.

"Now, let the guests arrive," said he. "Refreshment's ready."

"They're almost here," she whispered presently. "See there?"

Cautiously they peeked over the solid iron bulwark, and started with surprise. The Guinea men had loomed up almost in a moment from the night. The bulks of their long canoes were adumbrated by the guttering torches at each prow, surging upward, dipping, sliding over the hungry, lapping tongues of sea. Swarming they came. Everywhere flicked a swash of paddle-blades, everywhere swung innumerable black bodies in rhythm with the crooning plunder-song. The drums were silent, all save one that pulsed incessantly.

With a flesh-tingling wail of dissonance, the Guinea blacks teemed up about the Sutherland. A hum and murmur of barbaric voices filled the night. The acrid smoke from the torches stung the watchers' nostrils as they crouched, gripping their rifles.

"See," whispered Willard. "They're boarding now."

A sullen glow blurred up behind the port-rail midships. Then a blotch of flame wounded the shadows, and by this raw, wind-lashed beacon they saw the wreckers scramble in herds across the rail, their black, muscular bodies gleaming with sweat. Lights glinted from steel blades and spearheads.

"Armed for bloody work!" thought Willard, but he held his peace.

They clotted in a shifting mass, with cries like beasts; cracked, wild laughter; gibberish. And still they came, and came, and came.

"Heavens, what an onslaught!" Willard groaned. "It seems a shame to wait."

"Maybe they'll never think of coming aft?" breathed the girl.

"Heaven knows! They're in the saloon now. Hark! They're plundering — looking for the dead!"

Lights gleamed from the windows; noises rose within. The ship swarmed like a gigantic anthill, with this fetid crew. And now the watchers saw numberless black fellows crowding to the rail with loot, tossing it to waiting canoe-men. The whole scene blent and ran together like a nightmare. Ethel shut her eyes to it, bowed her head and waited.

"Ready!"

The doctor's hissed command aroused her. With sudden paralyzing dread she looked. A mob of the cursed ghouls were scouting toward them up the gangway.

Blear-faced and hideous they came, peering with brandished torches for what they might find. Ethel saw their little evil eyes; their red-dyed teeth as they grinned, jabbering; their shovel-headed spears.

"Now!" yelled the doctor. Night split wide-open with the fire from their rifles; crackling echoes smashed back from the cabin. Ethel looked.

She saw a struggling, screaming ruck that fled, a tangled heap jammed in the gangway — a heap that quivered.

There was no time for looking. Into her hands the doctor thrust another rifle.

"At the thick of 'em!" he shouted, and again death spouted from the barricade. Up to the sky shrilled a chorus of mad fear, so poignant, so unspeakable that they knew the rout was utter.

The wreckers made no stand. They lunged off in ripe clusters from the rail, swam for their dear black lives, and lost full many. Some reached their fellows in the boats; cries, howls, demoniac execrations dwindled as the *barracas* foamed away.

The doctor wiped his face with a torn sleeve and stood erect.

"They'll be back soon," said he. "Stay here; I'm going to investigate. If I whistle, look alive for orders."

He pressed a revolver into her hand, clambered the barricade and was gone. The darkness swallowed him.

She crouched behind the barricade, waiting, wondering, thrilling with the first imperative command which ever, as a woman, had been given her. The mastery of it steadied her, and was sweet. It almost made her forget the aching shoulder where the rifle-butt had plunged, and the dizzy swimming of her head.

The moments lagged eternal. What if some evil chance should fall and he should never come? She trembled at the thought. Suddenly and for the first time in her whole life she realized what manner of thing the comradeship of man may be, how very needful, very dear.

"Come back! Come back!" her lips formed the words there in the night — words which she dared not bring to utterance.

She heard a sudden wild noise on the sea. "They're coming back!" she shuddered.

Then, all at once, sounded a clear, low whistle on the starboard side.

"Drop a line here, and make it fast!" a voice rose up to her.

Not understanding, just obeying with a strange, new happiness in her fear, she tugged a rope from the tangled barricade, cross-looped it firmly on a chock, and flung it overboard. She heard it swish and strike the water — felt it tauten. The voice rose again: "First-rate, so far. I'm coming up!"

She peered across the rail. From the wreckers' fleet a nearing tumult wafted. The torches now were blazing not five hundred fathoms off.

"Hurry!" she cried. "Hurry, or it will be too late!"

Staring down into the dark, she could just see a dim mass toiling up the rope. Then, quite suddenly, the doctor swarmed to the rail — was over it.

"We've got to rush!" he panted. "Found a mighty handy craft banging at the end of a liana-cord — obliging of 'em to have left it! By dropping off to starboard, they may never know we're gone; at least, not till we've made a start. You gather up the cartridges. We're apt to need 'em. I'll take the guns."

She filled her bosom with the leaden deaths, while he, with his knife, slit out a square of tarpaulin, wrapped the guns in it, and lashed them with a cord. He made a loop and slung the bundle over his head.

Then a match r-r-rasped, and eager little flames licked at the barricade, fingering the oil-soaked cabin wall.

"Good-by, old Suth!" the doctor whispered hoarsely to himself.

A moment there was silence — then the doctor faced her.

"Come!" said he. "Come, now! Are you afraid?"

"Afraid — with you?"

VI.

AND IT BEFELL that, just before the breaking of the day, a man and woman, all disheveled, weary, black with powder-grime, resting on their paddles in a huge, uncouth *barraca*, turned and gazed back over the heaving ocean-breast to the distant tower of flame that bloodied the horizon.

Neither spoke. There was no need of words as the swift dawn flared up the sky. The sea crimsoned; fantom blues and opals spread abroad; luminous greens rimmed the far crescent of the western heaven as the last few watchful stars faded in the glory of another day.

"See?" said the man, pointing ahead.

The woman from her place in the bow looked far across the painted waters where a thin-drawn blur of smoke trailed slowly landward.

"See there? Two hours more and we'll be with — well, people again. Two hours more, and this will all be over, all be at an end for me — everything. I know how it will be! Just as I said last night, things will seem different to you — by the light of day. It is useless for me to hope otherwise."

"No, no," she answered, while her paddle dragged. "Not Africa — not you!"

As the full broad circle of the sun kissed the sea suddenly to gold, a song rose to the man's brave, eager lips. Strongly he plunged his paddle, urging the long *barraca* northward up the coast of Africa, over the bosom of the morning sea.

A WORTH-WHILE CRIME

"It LOOKS TO ME like a very ordinary sort of case," declared T. Ashley, tilting back his desk chair in the little office-and-laboratory place of his, whereof the door showed the sign in gold letters:

T. ASHLEY

INVESTIGATIONS

"Ordinary!" echoed Scanlon. "You call it ordinary when 'Big Boss' Hanrahan himself gets touched for seventeen thousand? I call it most extraordinary, I do. Hanged if I don't!"

"Oh, I don't mean that part of it," T. Ashley disclaimed, a trace of a smile curving his austere lips. "That particular angle of the affair possesses no interest for me. The personality of the victim, his affiliations, his control of the city's political machine are matters wholly beside the point, so far as I'm concerned. All I'm looking at, from the standpoint of my profession, is the technique of the crook. And this case presents no original factors there."

The September sunshine through his office window that overlooked the unending come-and-go of Albermarle Avenue, showed amused lines about the investigator's shrewd, keen gray eyes. Evidently he found Scanlon's agitation diverting.

"It's all quite a routine sort of thing," he added.

"Maybe 'tis," admitted Scanlon. "But there'll be somethin' infernally out o' the routine happen if that quick-touch artist ain't rounded up, P.D.Q.!"

"Indeed? Well, why did Hanrahan send you to me, then? I'm not what is known as a fast worker. I proceed with rather marked deliberation. Why didn't the boss turn this matter over to the bureau of criminal investigation?"

"And have every double-blanked paper in town full of it? Have every cop in the burg wise to it? Have the whole city laughin' up its sleeve at the boss? What's this here practical psychology I'm hearin' about, these days?"

"Of course," said T. Ashley. "I see. Ridicule can certainly kill a man, where all the 'uplift' attacks in the world would rattle off like peas from a rhinoceros. Yes, yes, I understand." Contemplatively he tapped the cover of an anthropological society's report. "So I'm to 'get' this malefactor for you in a private and inconspicuous manner. I'm to round up this genius, who's been clever enough to rob a — er —"

"A robber," Scanlon finished the phrase. "Say it, if you want to! That's what most o' the papers in town have been printin' for years. You got the idea, an' got it right. How much you want for the job?"

"The investigation," said T. Ashley, correcting him. "Well, Mr. Scanlon, my fee varies according to the interest I take in a case. Big interest, small fee. Enough interest, no fee at all. Slight interest, large fee. No interest at all —"

"You're frank, ain't you?" interrupted the boss's henchman. "That's *somethin'*. I figger, judgin' from the sympathy you feel for the boss, you'll want about five hundred bucks for tacklin' this case."

"A thousand," said T. Ashley dryly.

"Whew!" And Scanlon rubbed a shaven chin. "Well, if that's the best you can say —"

"It is. And not a contingent fee, either. I shall collect that thousand whether I succeed or not. Though in justice to myself I must say that I have still to record a failure. Agreed? Thank you. Now then, let us get back to the evidence. You say there was a window broken in Hanrahan's house by the crook?"

"Yep. A pane was busted out in the room where the safe is. The crook get in over the porch, there."

"Does anybody know about that broken pane?"

"Only the boss's boss."

"You refer to Mrs. Hanrahan?"

"Sure. And the fact that there's a playground nex' door, where the kids play baseball, makes that busted window a cinch to explain. Nobody knows about the 'touch' but me and the boss. He's havin' the pane reset today."

"The robbery," asked T. Ashley, "took place last night, while

Mr. and Mrs. Hanrahan were at the theater?"

"That's what."

"You saved the broken pieces of glass, naturally?"

"Surest little thing you know! I handled 'em with gloves, too, an' brought 'em along with me."

"Good! And then —"

"Well, the crook just opened the gopher, that's all, an' cleaned it like he'd had a vacuum cleaner."

"He didn't use force, I believe you said? No 'soup' or thermite. No tools."

"Nope. He just juggled the knob, that's all."

"I see. Well," and T. Ashley pondered a moment, pencil, in hand, "I'll take a run out and look the ground over this afternoon. But — let's see the glass, first."

Scanlon drew a flat package from his pocket, undid a string, opened the package, and spread out various bits of broken glass on the desk. He took good care not to touch them with his fingers, but poked them with a penholder to separate them.

"Very good, indeed," said T. Ashley. He took pincers from a tray, with which he seized the pieces one by one and examined them. Putting a jeweler's loupe into his eye, he gave them a more detailed inspection, turning them a little this way and that to vary the light across their surfaces.

"H'm!" he said at last, while Scanlon watched him with keen attention, his full-lidded blue eyes squinting a little. "This is altogether *too* easy. Yes, yes, indeed. Why, there are prints enough here to convict a regiment!"

"That's how I jiggered it'd be."

"Too bad you couldn't have turned this case over to the bureau. The whole thing is simplicity itself. You could have saved the boss a clean thousand, and he needs the money. That's his motto, isn't it — 'I need the money!'"

"We all need the money these days," returned Scanlon. "But other things has got to be reckoned, too. We don't want no public officials a-tall to get hep to this. Some way it'd leak if I was to give any of 'em a crack at these prints. All the boss wants now is to nab this bird, see, an' do it without makin' no roar. The boss is a bearcat for gettin' back at any guy that passes him the dinkum oil. Oh, he's a wise old kick, all right, the boss is!"

"So I understand," said T. Ashley. "But he can't get back at this bird, as you call the malefactor, without exposing the break and bringing down ridicule on himself. The minute that the bird is arrested —"

"Arrested? Who said anythin' about arrestin' him?" And Scanlon laughed twistedly. "*He* ain't goin' to be arrested! There's better ways to get a bird than by arrestin' him, an' you can pin that in your lid!"

"I suppose so. Well, that's none of my affair. My undertaking is just to earn my fee by locating the bird. After that, what happens to him is none of my affair."

"I see you've got me cold. You *can* locate him, can't you, with fingerprints like those?"

T. Ashley laughed a little scornfully. "By the way," he added, "now that I've looked these over, I don't think it will be necessary for me to visit Mr. Hanrahan's house. That would be 'gilding the lily,' you understand."

"Doing what to the which?"

"Pardon me. I mean, taking too much pains. I must say this so-called bird has been unusually liberal about leaving us his calling cards. I repeat that this affair is most ordinary. It's so easy as to possess hardly the interest of an ordinary, common or garden variety of murder. Still, as I've agreed to take it on, I'll go through with it."

"And you'll call me up?"

"As soon," promised T. Ashley, "as I have this predatory person's name, age, description, record, and present address. After that —"

"*We'll* look out for the 'after that' part of it!" exclaimed Scanlon grimly.

"Quite so. But I tell you now, you're gunning for small game. A modern 'house prowler' who doesn't know enough to wear gloves must be deficient, indeed. Poor game!"

"All the more reason why the boss can't afford to let such a guy run round loose an' get away with it," said Scanlon. "Supposin' it should leak that a third-rater had —"

"Of course. Well, I'll let you know. I'll phone you at your office. Let's see, now — Scanlon Paving and Contracting Co., isn't it?"

"That's me. Well, thanks!" Scanlon stood up and extended his hand. But T. Ashley, already once more bending over the fragments of glass, apparently did not see it. "Well — good day."

"Oh, *good*-day!"

When Scanlon was gone, and the door closed, T. Ashley leaned back and smiled.

"Vanity," said he, "thy name is man!"

II.

THE MESSAGE SCANLON received over the wire several days later vastly astonished him.

"Hello there! Scanlon? . . . Yes, T. Ashley speaking. I say, Scanlon, what the deuce do you mean by trying to amuse yourself at my expense? . . . Don't understand, eh? The devil you don't! Practical jokes are all very well, but — what's that you say? . . . Oh, yes, I'll tell you, all right enough. . . . Yes, any time you like; the sooner the better. Have I *what*? . . . Found *out*? Good-by!"

The slam of the receiver onto the hook left Scanlon vastly amazed.

"Well, what d'you know about that?" he asked himself. "What's he vaporin' about now, I'd like to know? Can you beat it? Has that bird gone cuckoo all of a sudden, or what?"

He took his Panama and departed from the office of the Scanlon Paving and Contracting Co. in more of a hurry than he had been for weeks.

"I tell you, I don't get you a-tall," he insisted, when he and T. Ashley were alone together in the little laboratory office overlooking Albermarle Avenue. "Anybody'd think, from what you just now shot over the wire at me, that I'd been tryin' to feed you some phony stuff!"

"And anybody would be quite correct in that assumption," returned T. Ashley. His jaw looked tight, his eye hostile. "I suppose, from your point of view, it's an excellent witticism, trying to make sport of a private investigator."

"What d'you mean? Come across!"

"Of course, the department is out to knife a man who's proved them lunkheads half a dozen times. That's quite comprehensible. But

I hardly thought the Big Boss himself — and you — would be quite so childish. Another thing: you forget that in trying to bring me into ridicule," and T. Ashley struck the desk a blow with his fist, "you two may get involved worse than I am! That would be a horse of another color!"

"What d'you mean, horse? All the horse I see, round here, is on *me!*"

And Scanlon shook a puzzled head. He let both hands fall, palms outward.

"Who instigated this, anyhow?" demanded T. Ashley.

"Here's where I quit!" said Scanlon. "I'd better beat it while my shoes are good. Maybe *you* know what you're talkin' about, but darned if I do!"

"You — you mean to say you really don't understand?"

"Well, you heard me the first time!"

"You don't know what kind of a wild-goose chase you've been putting me up against?"

"How many more times d'you want me to say it? Bring a stack o' Bibles, or something and —"

"But, what the deuce?" exclaimed T. Ashley. "Whoever in the world gave you those fingerprints?"

"Nobody! Get that straight, now. I rounded up them prints myself. The boss called me out to his house and told me about the break, and I —"

"Do you mean to tell me," and T. Ashley's eyes narrowed, "that those prints, to the best of your knowledge and belief, were really made by the man who robbed Mr. Hanrahan's safe?"

"That's the way it rides, s'help me! Why?"

"*Why?* Oh, by the Lord Harry, now, that's flogging it! Look at that, will you?"

And T. Ashley with a flirt of the wrist tossed over a letter on his desk for Scanlon to read. He added, in a tone vastly far from his usual suavity:

"See what McDonald, of the Federal identification bureau at Leavenworth has to say about it. *Somebody* has been having a devil of a joke with somebody. Now then, who is it — and why?"

Scanlon caught up the letter.

Dear Mr. Ashley: Reporting on the microphotographs of the prints, let me say they have been identified as those of Peter W. Blau, alias Dutch Pete, alias The Grayback. His number on our records is 143,297. Will send Bertillon if desired. Very truly yours,

M. S. McDonald.

Scanlon reread the letter before looking up. Then he asked, puzzled. "Well, that's all right, ain't it? That's straight dope. What's all the roar you're sendin' across?"

"What's it about? Oh, I say, now!"

"I don't see nothin' phony about this! All it looks like, from where I stand, is the first move toward landin' this here Dutch Pete guy in the big house, and —"

"Is *that* all it looks like, to you?" demanded T. Ashley, with mordant scorn. "Well, now, where do you suppose I'd have to look to find that man?"

"How the devil should I know? That's your job!"

"My job, eh? A job for sextons, you mean! And I'm not in the pick-and-shovel brigade — not just yet."

Scanlon regarded him with eyes of astonishment.

"Come on, come on!" he exclaimed. "Shoot it across, clean, and get it off your chest! What d'you mean, pick-and-shovel brigade?"

"I mean," answered T. Ashley with emphasis on every word, "that this Peter W. Blau, alias Dutch Pete, alias The Grayback, was electrocuted nearly six months ago!"

III.

NOW IT WAS Scanlon's turn to flush with anger.

"You must be bats!" he exclaimed. "What kind of a gag are you tryin' to slip over on me, anyhow?"

"No gag at all, to quote your own choice language! And as for being 'bats,' I'm not so crazy as to assert that a dead man can get up out of his grave and go gallivanting round the country robbing safes!"

"I never said nothin' like that!"

"The deuce you didn't! You brought me a dead man's fingerprints, with the preposterous assertion that —"

"I brought you the prints that was on that there pane out to the boss's house. The man that made them prints cleaned that gopher!"

"Of course. Well, you'd better tell that to the spirits."

"Don't know any. Where are they?"

"Never mind."

"McDonald — he's made a slip-up, that's all. He got them prints doped wrong."

"McDonald never gets anything wrong!" And T. Ashley thumped the desk again. "The modern science of fingerprinting never makes a mistake. Out of all the millions of prints in the world, there are no —"

"Oh, yes, I know all about that. I'm hep. You don't have to flash no lecture on fingerprints on me! All I'm sayin' is that if Mac 'made' them prints as a guy's that croaked six months ago, either he's made a misplay or you're wrong."

"Wrong about what?"

"About this here Dutch Pete bein' dead."

T. Ashley jerked open a drawer of his desk, took out a letter, shoved it at Scanlon.

"How about *that*?" demanded he.

Scanlon glanced at the signature. "From Warden Hotchkiss, eh?" said he. "Prestonville pen?"

"Yes. If you want proof —"

"'Murder, first degree — '" read Scanlon. "'Electrocuted, February 17th, 1922.' Well, that's official, all O.K."

"Rather!"

"So then there's only one answer."

"You mean," demanded T. Ashley, "two men had the same name?"

"Looks like it."

"Nothing of the kind happened in *this* case. When I got that word from Hotchkiss, I made another set of microphotographs and sent them to him. He wasn't long in reporting. I just today got this letter from him."

"What's he say?"

"Read it for yourself!" And T. Ashley handed over another letter. Amazed, Scanlon read:

The prints submitted have been carefully
verified by comparison with our records.
They are those of the man you refer to, viz.:
Peter W. Blau.

For a moment Scanlon paused, his brow knit. A dry smile curved the lips of T. Ashley.

"Ye gods, I — I don't get this at all!" admitted Scanlon, beginning to weaken.

"Oh, I see you're waking up to the situation, at last," declared T. Ashley. "You understand, don't you, that this report absolutely eliminates the double-identity hypothesis?"

"Sure, sure. Well, then, the only flash I can take at it is that some fresh guy — but, no, *that* couldn't be!"

"You mean, somebody may have given you some prints of this Dutch Pete's, made before his execution?"

"Nobody *could* of," insisted Scanlon, his mind a daze. "Why, I picked up them pieces of glass myself at the boss's house!"

"Well, then," concluded T. Ashley, "those pieces were 'planted' there by somebody, for some purpose that, frankly, is beyond me."

"Not a-tall! Some o' them prints was on pieces o' glass that still stuck in the window sash. I put on a pair o' gloves, careful, an' worked 'em loose, myself. Wrapped 'em up, never touchin' 'em with my own bare fingers, and brought 'em to you, without ever openin' 'em."

"Then that package was changed somewhere on the way."

Scanlon laughed, with tense nerves. "You're pretty good now an' then, Ashley," said he, "but once in a while you don't even hit the outside ring. That there package never left my pocket from the time I shoved it in there till I laid it on this here desk!"

"I tell you there must have been some substitution, somewhere along the line."

"And I tell you there wasn't! Say, I even remember the shape of some o' them pieces. I'll go on any stand in this country an' swear I give you the very identical pieces I started with."

"But in that case —"

"Well, what?"

"Hang it, Scanlon, we're confronted by an insoluble mystery! A set of circumstances contrary to reason — a staring impossibility!"

"Impossibilities has always been your specialty," uttered Scanlon, not without malice. "At least, anybody'd think so, the way you count yourself in on the Get There Club. D'you mean to say you're ready to quit?"

"Quit?" demanded T. Ashley. "I haven't begun yet!"

IV.

T. ASHLEY HAD NO success whatever with his investigation. No train of reasoning could lead him beyond what seemed a blank wall barring the path of deduction. Putting aside the supernatural as a factor in which he had no faith, he found himself confronted by a sphinx to whose question there was no Oedipus to bring an answer.

A visit to Hanrahan's house and an examination of the safe itself yielded nothing but more prints, all made by the man who six months before had paid the extreme penalty of the law in Prestonville penitentiary.

"Well, I'm hanged!" exclaimed T. Ashley to himself, and when he, always loath to give up, had been forced to such a statement, matters had reached a desperate pitch.

They became more desperate still, however, when, ten days later, Scanlon returned to the laboratory office with this petrifying news: "Sam Levitsky's apartment, out in Maplewold, has been touched to the tune of thirty-three thousand!"

"So?" demanded T. Ashley. "Well now, this is getting interesting, I must say!"

"Too interesting!" said Scanlon. "It's another crack at the boss, you see."

"Yes, yes, I suppose so. It's practically the same as a direct attack on Hanrahan — for what belongs to the boss is the boss's, and what belongs to Levitsky is the boss's, too. At least, so runs popular rumor."

"Cor-rect," Scanlon agreed. "Though that's just between you an' I. All part of the same job, what? Prob'ly same guy?"

"I'll have to look the ground over, before expressing any opinion as to that. But I should say it was all part of the original campaign. I'll be liberal with you, for the sake of science, and consider this as part of the same case, at the same fee. The fact is," added T. Ashley, "my professional interest is aroused. I'd like to know *who* has public spirit enough to direct an attack against Hanrahan & Co."

"I judge you ain't strong for the boss, yourself."

"Not perceptibly — especially since he killed that appropriation for the orthopedic hospital, and —"

"Now look here," interrupted Scanlon, "he *had* to do that. If he hadn't, that silk-stockin' gang of goo-goos would of —"

"I'm not arguing municipal politics with you," disclaimed T. Ashley, raising his hand. "All I'm doing is expressing an opinion. That opinion won't interfere with my professional duties. I propose that we take a run out to Maplewold and look over the ground. Were there any traces left — that is, traces visible to you?"

"No. Nothin' broken this time. A slicker job than the other."

"Practice makes perfect," said T. Ashley, "even for a dead man." He took his hat. "Well, let's get along."

"The quicker — an' the quieter — the better!" Scanlon declared.

At the scene of the second robbery, T. Ashley carefully examined the premises, while Levitsky poured out invective and Scanlon adjured him to hold his peace. Levitsky's third-floor apartment was in "The Rosalind," facing Grosvenor Park. Entrance had been effected through the dining-room window that gave upon a fire escape overlooking the alley. Nothing had been broken. The window catch had been pushed back with a slender blade, and the sash raised.

Fingerprints were plentiful on the combination of the wall safe, which had been closed again after the touch, but these prints impinged upon each other and were confused to such an extent that even though T. Ashley brought them up with developing powder and then studied them attentively under his best glass, he could make little of them.

"I've got to have something more definite than *those*," said he, and instituted a painstaking search. After a few minutes, during which Scanlon and Levitsky partly drowned their chagrin in certain strong waters, T. Ashley exclaimed, "Ah!"

"Got a lead, have you?" demanded Scanlon.

T. Ashley's only answer was: "Have you got a keyhole saw, a hammer, and a chisel?"

"I can get 'em for you," said Levitsky. "What's de idea?"

"Get them, then."

When they had been brought from janitorial regions, T. Ashley cut a section from the varnished window sill. This he wrapped in clean paper.

"That's all I need," said he. "Let's get back to the office, now."

Together, T. Ashley and Scanlon returned to town, leaving the Big Boss's henchman under injunctions of strictest secrecy.

V.

"THIS IS POSITIVELY the most amazing thing I was ever confronted with!" exclaimed the investigator, after he had subjected the piece of window sill to exhaustive comparison with his microphotographs.

"What d'you mean, most amazin' thing?" demanded Scanlon, chewing on an extinct cigar. He spoke a little thickly now, by reason of Levitsky's good cheer.

"Our old friend, Blau — Dutch Pete — is back on the job again."

"No!"

"Fact. Prints don't lie."

"You mean — that dead man's prints are on that piece o' sill?"

"That's exactly what I mean!"

Silence followed. From below, on Albermarle Avenue, rose the confused but cheerful rumble of the city's traffic, the hymn of life; but in the office something cold and numbing seemed to weigh and settle — the spirit of death that would not die.

All at once Scanlon, now completely sobered, exclaimed: "Le' *me* have a look at them prints!"

"Oh, you wouldn't know! All prints look alike to the untrained man. But to the expert every whorl, volute, and ridge is as distinctive under the glass as a human face — more so, because even the best man now and then is fooled by a chance resemblance. Even the Bertillon itself now and then goes wrong. But no two prints, from infancy to old age, are ever alike — and they never change. I have here," T. Ashley added, tapping the piece of window sill with a metal probe, "excellent prints of the fore and middle fingers of the Levitsky burglar's right hand."

"And they're the same as on the glass I took from the boss's?"

"Absolutely."

"Well, I *will* be darned!"

"It looks as if we'd both be darned," said T. Ashley cynically. "Your job and my reputation are both at stake, and — barring an admission that spiritualists and all that ilk are right — we seem to have come to the end of our tether."

Again he applied his lens to a set of microphotographs of the prints left on the smooth-varnished Levitsky window sill, and fell to studying them intently. For a moment he made no sign, but all at once his attention tautened. He bent closer, adjusting the glass.

"H'm!"

"What's up, now?" asked Scanlon, forgetting even to chew on the extinct cigar.

"Oh, you wouldn't understand."

"Well, le' me look, anyhow. I guess the boss is payin' enough for this job, so I'm entitled to at least a flash!"

"By all means," admitted T. Ashley, giving place to Scanlon.

"Some map!" commented Scanlon. "Looks like a plan o' Boston, or some place. Who'd ever think a man ever had all them lines on the ends o' his fingers?"

"Nobody, except an intelligent person," replied the investigator with caustic emphasis. "And by the way, you know, apes have just the same kind of lines, too, thus proving our relationship with our backward cousins."

"Can the deep stuff!" said Scanlon. "All I'm interested in, now, is these here lines belongin' to Dutch Pete. So a dead man made them prints, did he?"

"He did, unless the whole modern science of fingerprinting is fallible."

"Come again?"

"I mean, unless it can make mistakes, which it never has been known to do, yet. That's its whole value, its absolute accuracy. And what it says, now, is that the prints left in both robberies were produced by a man who went to the electric chair — and was killed there — the seventeenth of last February."

"Well, I *am* hanged!"

"So you've already said, and I think it quite likely. Seen enough, have you?"

"Yep." And Scanlon left the instrument. "Looks like we was up against the cushion, hard, an' no way to bounce."

T. Ashley rubbed his chin, saying nothing. His thoughts, however, were: "There's no such thing as an inexplicable phenomenon. Facts leave traces, and traces can't lie. At the bottom of every 'hopeless' problem there's some simple, obvious explanation. So then, all I've got to do is —"

"Don't strain yourself with thinkin' too much," Scanlon interrupted his cogitation with sarcasm. He reached for his hat. "When you figger it out how a dead one can blow back an' go to work as a boxman, let me know."

"I'll let you know, all right. And meantime, warn your fat friend, Levitsky, to keep quiet."

"No danger of *his* belchin'. He'll be mum as the boss himself. But the quicker you get some goods to show, the better. The boss ain't noted much for patience."

"He may have to acquire one virtue, at least," remarked T. Ashley. "Good-day!"

Alone, the investigator resumed his study through the lens. For a long time he sat there, examining the newly discovered factor which, at first glimpse, had caused him to give utterance to that "H'm!" of slight wonder.

After a while he got up, went to his bookcase, and brought back to his desk a heavy volume in French — Henri de Brissac's *Traité de la Peau, Humaine et Animale*.

He spent an hour over this monumental work on human and animal skins, carefully examining the colored plates and here or there dipping into the text.

At last he put up the book, lighted a cigar, and locked his office door. From now on, till such time as pleased him, T. Ashley had become invisible, inaccessible.

He lay down on his broad couch in the laboratory office, smoked, studied the ceiling, pondered. At last, after two cigars had become lamentable butts, he reached for the phone, called Warden

Hotchkiss at the Prestonville penitentiary, and by long distance made an appointment for next morning. "Dutch Pete," said he to himself, after he had hung up the receiver again, "I rather think I'll have to find out a little more about you!"

VI.

TWO DAYS LATER T. Ashley called on Doctor Holden K. Dillingham, at the doctor's office in the Monadnock Building, on Franchot Street. The doctor, T. Ashley noted, was smallish, trim, shaven, going a bit bald, and possessed of keen blue eyes, a trifle prominent, also a chin that promised: "What I undertake, I do."

"Well, sir?" asked Dillingham when he was alone with his caller — a new patient, doubtless, thought he.

"I believe you're the physician who has been interested in getting the new orthopedic hospital for children started out in the Sheridan Boulevard district?" asked T. Ashley.

"Why, yes. In fact," added the doctor, "I'm chairman of the organization board."

"I might," said T. Ashley, "have a contribution to make to that enterprise, under certain circumstances."

"That's good news," said Dillingham. "We can certainly use a little help. This town's in crying need of such an institution."

"So I understand. Too bad the city wouldn't meet the board's proposition as stated some time ago in the papers."

"You mean our offer to put up one hundred thousand dollars, if the city would contribute fifty thousand dollars, and make it a semi-public institution?"

"Exactly. But what else can anybody expect," asked T. Ashley, "with men like Hanrahan and Levitsky pulling the puppet strings and working for their own pockets instead of the public welfare?"

"What else, indeed?"

"Men like that can always be counted on to block any forward-looking move. They're not merely content with throwing sticks in the wheel of progress, but they rob the taxpayers right and left."

"Correct," agreed the doctor.

"By the way," said T. Ashley, changing the subject, "what do you think of this?"

He drew from his inside coat pocket a sheet of paper and spread it on the doctor's desk. Dillingham put on his glasses, looked at it a moment, and then, with the slightest suggestion of a frown, replied: "I don't quite understand you. Are you asking for my opinion of this rather highly magnified fingerprint?"

T. Ashley bent forward, pointing with the tip of a pencil. "What do you make of that?" asked he.

"Of what?"

"This mark, here, a little to the left of the middle of the print."

"It — well, it looks like a scar, to me."

"Yes, so it does — superficially. Have you no other opinion, doctor?"

"I don't understand you," said Dillingham. "Are you here to talk hospital or fingerprints?"

"A little of both, maybe."

"I mean, is this a professional or a nonprofessional call?"

"Oh, highly professional on both sides, I assure you!"

"You're talking in riddles, I must say," said the doctor. "Well, I'm used to riddles. I get lots of them in my practice. Every doctor does."

"But few," declared T. Ashley, "solve their riddles with the proverbial 'neatness and dispatch' that characterize you. Let us now return to the matter of this fingerprint. Would you say, doctor, that this mark — here, on the print — was made by a scar?"

"Looks like it," said the doctor. His fingers began to drum a bit nervously on his chair arm, but quickly stopped.

"Ah, but look closer."

"Well, then?"

"Study the print with a magnifying glass, if you have one handy."

The doctor, seeming altogether mystified, opened a drawer of his desk, took out a glass, and examined the print.

"That mark certainly looks like a scar to me," he declared.

"In a scar, however," objected T. Ashley, "the edges would be smoothly healed. Here, you see, they are rough. And, moreover, there are several marks — in the scar itself — that look like tiny, wandering chains. Concatenated markings, to be technical."

"Well, what of it?" demanded Dillingham. He seemed a bit

impatient.

"As a physician, you know that scar tissue presents no such markings."

"True enough. But what in the world are you driving at, Mr. Ashley? This is all very puzzling, I must say." The doctor frowned. "First you talk hospital, and speak of a donation. Then you catechize me about fingerprints, and now — well, what are you coming at, anyhow?"

"At the obvious conclusion that this mark, here on this fingerprint, was not produced by a scar at all, but by another kind of skin altogether from human skin."

"I don't seem to follow you," said the doctor, laying down his magnifying glass.

"To state it still more plainly," expounded T. Ashley, "when the original fingerprint was made, from which this microphotograph was taken, there was another piece of skin — a nonhuman skin — under the skin that made the print."

"Oh, a graft, perhaps?" said Dillingham, as if an idea had occurred to him.

"No — though this whole matter is connected with one, to pardon a colloquialism. There are no signs of growths, adhesions, or anything of that kind. In fact, both skins from which this print was made were dead skins."

"Dead?"

"Quite so. And, as I have said before, the smaller piece of skin was not human at all."

"But I don't understand. If not human, what then?"

"The skin of an animal. To be more accurate, a dog."

VII.

DOCTOR DILLINGHAM'S eyes fell. A slight moisture covered his forehead; but then, the day was very warm.

"This is all quite beyond my comprehension," said he. "And, moreover, why are you telling me these details? What do you want of me?"

"Ah, that," said T. Ashley, "will develop later. For the moment, let me tell you a little story. A simple, unvarnished tale. Do you mind if I smoke?"

"Not at all. I'll join you."

T. Ashley lighted a cigar; the doctor, a pipe. T. Ashley by no means failed to note the tremor of Doctor Dillingham's hand as the match hung above the pipe bowl, but the doctor smiled and said: "A good story is always acceptable, though I must confess you've got me mystified. This is certainly an odd consultation."

"It's an odd case," declared T. Ashley. "The story is even more so — but a capital one. It begins with the electrocution of a notorious stickup man and murderer, Peter W. Blau, alias Dutch Pete, and so forth, last February, at Prestonville."

"Well?" asked the doctor, trying to look at T. Ashley.

"Well, Dutch Pete's body remained unclaimed, and was handed over for dissection to a certain medical school, which I won't name. So much I know. From this point on I shall fill in, with deductions, certain gaps which occur between the established facts. You see, I am quite frank with you. I'm showing you my whole box of tricks."

"This is certainly mystifying!" murmured the doctor.

"Is it not? But vastly instructive. Let us, however, not go into side issues. Let us stick to the fate and fortunes of Dutch Pete, who in death has been destined to carry on his chosen profession in a most extraordinary manner, though perhaps to quite a different end than any he himself would have chosen."

"I'm sure," said Dillingham, "this is all most incomprehensible."

"You'll soon understand. A certain physician and surgeon connected with the above-unmentioned medical school got possession of Dutch Pete's hands — possibly in connection with some research work regarding the characteristics of criminal types."

"Interesting!" commented the doctor, blowing much smoke.

"Is it not?"

"And what part of the story are you telling me now?" asked Dillingham. "Fact or inference?"

"Inference. Deduction, I should say. You'll soon see where the deduction hitches on to solid fact again. Now, it so happened that this same physician was a leading spirit in a proposed public improvement, the carrying out of which was blocked by a couple of sinister, predatory individuals. The doctor conceived the idea — very intelligent idea, indeed, and showing real imagination as well as a sense of poetic justice — of enlisting the help of a dead crook to beat a couple of live crooks."

"Just how could that be?" asked Dillingham.

"Let me explain. This doctor must at some previous period of his career have had considerable mechanical experience. He certainly knew much about the mechanism of safes. Also he realized that his profession was an excellent shield. A doctor, you know, can go almost anywhere without exciting suspicion. He can carry tools in his medical bag. He can leave his car standing anywhere. In a good many ways he enjoys rather an unusual freedom of movement, coming and going as he will, especially at night, without any one thinking ill of it. So far, so good."

"And what then?" asked Dillingham, relighting his pipe which had gone out.

"This particular physician I have in mind," continued T. Ashley, "chose direct action as his means of punishing the crooked and sinister forces in question, and also of forwarding the public improvement in which he was interested. You see I am speaking in non-specific terms. No names mentioned, of course. Being a cautious and very brainy man, he evolved the idea of covering his tracks in a manner that seemed absolutely beyond the reach of analytical reason."

"Nothing," murmured Dillingham, "seems beyond the reach of such analytical reason as you practice."

"Thank you. Never mind about that, however. You understand there are no personalities, on either side, in anything I'm telling you now."

"Certainly! Well, then?"

"The physician so arranged matters that, unless he were really caught in the act, his safety seemed assured."

"How very prescient of him!" commented Dillingham, forcing a smile.

"His idea," resumed T. Ashley, "was something like Robin Hood's — taking from thieves to give to the needy. Only he used modern science to help him, instead of a good crossbow and clothyard shafts. Unfortunately, however, he overlooked a trifling detail."

"A detail?"

"Yes. He failed to notice a slight cut, or tear, in one finger of one of his gloves."

"What gloves?"

"Gloves," said T. Ashley, "unlike any others in the whole world. Gloves made of the skin of the fingers of the deceased Dutch Pete, dissected from the dead hands and drawn on over a pair of thin other gloves."

"How very extraordinary!" The doctor's eyes blinked, narrowed.

"Is it not?"

"But how in the world could you ever manage to make up such a hypothetical narrative?"

"The microscope helps to some extent. That mark which shows in the print on your desk there is the mark of a cut or tear, as I have already told you. The fingerprint itself is that of Dutch Pete. The little bit of skin under the cut must have been dogskin. No other skin leaves just that kind of mark."

"Indeed?"

"Yes. The only answer is, double gloves. So it is all quite plain. And now," T. Ashley added, while Dillingham's face grew ever more and more drawn, "now I have a little proposition to make you."

"What — what proposition?"

"I am willing to become a participant in crime with the owner of that amazing pair of gloves."

"You — you mean —"

"In exchange for those gloves," said T. Ashley slowly, leaning forward and looking square at Dillingham, "in exchange for those gloves — which I will destroy, after having examined them — I will drop this whole investigation at once, and carry it no farther, now or at any future time."

"I — really, Mr. Ashley, I — don't understand you."

"Oh, yes you do! The thing done was legally criminal, but morally most praiseworthy. Hanrahan and Levitsky bilked you of fifty thousand. Your two 'touches' came to just that. They totaled exactly fifty. Another point I haven't overlooked. If you'd taken another dollar, you'd have been a thief yourself. As it is, you're a public benefactor; you deserve medals! Especially as this morning's paper carries that announcement from you that the success of the orthopedic is at last assured. So —"

"But I — I tell you —"

"Come, come!" said T. Ashley, laying a hand on Dillingham's arm. "Why not make a clean breast of it? Why not give me the gloves, in exchange for a Scotch verdict of 'Not guilty but don't do it again?'"

Dillingham tried to moisten his lips with a dry tongue. He managed to articulate: "No man — voluntarily — runs his head into a noose."

T. Ashley laughed, and it was rare for him to laugh. "Tell you what I'll do, to prove I'm on the level with you. Keep the gloves, if you want to. In fact, I rather think you'd better. There's one supremely good use you can make of them."

"And what's that?"

"Show them to me, and then I'll tell you."

The doctor hesitated a moment, smeared his sweating brow, then got up and walked to a filing cabinet at the other side of his office. T. Ashley noticed how his legs shook.

"You're making no mistake, my friend," he assured the doctor, "to trust me. If there's any man in this city who hates Hanrahan and Levitsky worse than you do, that man is myself."

"That's good enough for me," replied the doctor. He pulled out a drawer of the cabinet, reached far into the back of it, took something, and returned to the desk, exclaiming, "Here!"

He thrust into T. Ashley's hands a pair of thin dogskin gloves, the fingers of which were covered with human skin.

"Here," he repeated. "You win!"

"We both win," corrected T. Ashley, with keen interest examining the gloves. "You win immunity, and I win another triumph for my deductive methods — though it must be a secret one. But, after all, you see how very simple it all is, when one knows the method? Here, take them back." He tossed the gloves onto the desk. "My offer still stands. I happen to have a thousand dollars soon payable to me, for which I have no personal use. Will you accept that thousand, for the orthopedic?"

"*Will* I? Good God!"

"Also my suggestion as to disposing of these gloves?"

"What — what's that?"

"Wrap and seal them, and include them among the articles to be deposited in the metal box that goes into the corner stone of the hospital. For they *are* its corner stone!"

A moment the doctor stared at him. Then his hand hesitated toward that of the investigator.

T. Ashley shook hands with him warmly. "Agreed, then?"

But Dillingham, choking, could find no word.

VIII.

Next afternoon T. Ashley called Scanlon by phone. "It's about that matter, you know," said he.

"Oh, you got it doped out, have you?" Scanlon queried.

"I am very sorry to say I haven't. In fact, I have been obliged to drop the affair."

"The devil!"

"Just what I said, when I discovered that my charwoman had done a little cleaning up. The fact is, Scanlon, all the evidence in the case has disappeared."

"You don't expect me to believe nothin' like that!"

"I expect — and require — you to believe anything I choose to tell you!" T. Ashley's voice was decisive. "I repeat that the case is closed. You can give your employers the explanation I have just given you. Between you and me, however, I don't mind telling you it will be very much better for all parties concerned if things stop right where they are. I could go further — but decline. An interesting case, but circumstances have altered —"

"Oh, that's the way it rides, eh? Well now, by —"

"Yes, that's the way, Good-by!" T. Ashley hung up the receiver and smiled.

"They'll never dare refuse that thousand," he pondered. "I know too much. And they'll never dare try anybody else, even if they had any evidence left. I've got them frightened. It's all worked out very well. Very, very well indeed."

He pondered a moment, then added: "Next to handing that thousand to Dillingham, I rather think I'll enjoy the laying of that orthopedic corner stone!"

Then T. Ashley lighted still another cigar, and as the smoke ascended, smiled wisely to himself.

www.ingramcontent.com/pod-product-compliance
Lightning Source LLC
Chambersburg PA
CBHW050746250626
47155CB00005B/1945